D1028845
THIS
BOOK
BELONGS
TO
Sadie
wheeler

CAMELOT **JEROME BEATTY, JR.** has written several books for young people. A former newspaperman and magazine editor, his articles have appeared in many publications, including *The Saturday Review,* where he wrote the Trade Winds column. Born in New York, Mr. Beatty was graduated from Dartmouth College. He now lives on Cape Cod with his family.

Matthew Looney In The Outback

A space story by

JEROME BEATTY, JR.

Pictures by GAHAN WILSON

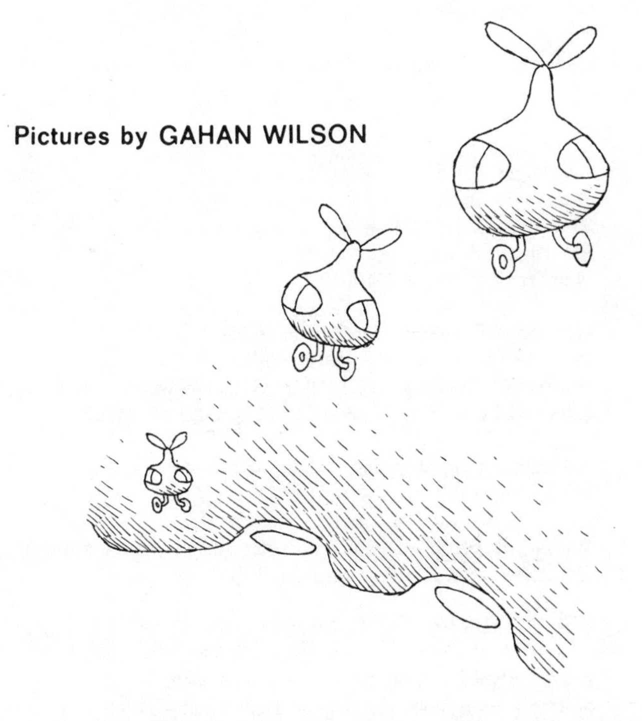

CAMELOT BOOKS/PUBLISHED BY AVON

AVON BOOKS
A division of
The Hearst Corporation
959 Eighth Avenue
New York, New York 10019

Published by arrangement with William R. Scott, Inc.

Library of Congress Catalog Card Number: 69-14567.

First Camelot Printing, February, 1973.

CAMELOT TRADEMARK REG. U.S. PAT. OFF. AND
FOREIGN COUNTRIES, REGISTERED TRADEMARK—
MARCA REGISTRADA, HECHO EN CHICAGO, U.S.A.

Printed in the U.S.A.

FOR THE LOYAL MEMBERS
OF THE CLUB

Table of Contents

1. Maria Makes Up Her Mind

"Maria! Maria Looney! Will you get the paper, please?"

Mrs. Looney's voice echoed through the cool corridors of the Looneys' comfortable cave dwelling on Zinc Road, Crater Plato, Moon. Maria went to the huge stone door, pulled at the handle and swung it open easily on its diamond hinges. She picked up the *Daily Mews* from the doorstep and carried it back to the kitchen, where her mother was whipping up a fancy luna-bean casserole for dinner.

"Any word?" Mrs. Looney asked.

Her daughter was already studying the front page seriously. "Yes. Tomorrow, Lunday, cold and clammy, with a chance of meteor showers on Marsday."

Her mother frowned. "Really, Maria, why read the weather report when it's your brother's circumstances we're concerned with? I'm worried. He might be in trouble."

"But I *was* thinking of Matthew, Mom. After all, tomorrow's Daddy's day off, and he promised to take us to Mooniversity Heights, so we could put in a call to the *Feebey*—weather permitting. Remember?"

"Of course, I remember, dear," her mother sighed, lighting the sulphur oven. "Now, how about looking for some news of the expedition."

"Okay. Let's see. Here it is. Gosh, they don't tell much, do they?"

"What does it say? What does it say?" her mother cried impatiently. Maria read from the paper:

SPACE SHIP ON COURSE

Commander of FEEBEY *Reports All Is Well*

Mooniversity Heights:—An interspatial dispatch from the space vehicle *Feebey* revealed today that the ship had moved 44 million lunacules closer to Moon, on its return from exploring the Hercules Globular Cluster.

"There has been no departure from our normal routine," said Admiral Lockhard Looney, leader of the cosmic flight, in an interspatial message to Space Expeditionary Headquarters here. He reported that their position was presently near the Horsehead Nebula.

"We expect to reach Moon on schedule," Admiral Looney predicted.

"They don't even mention Matthew's name," Mrs. Looney remarked sadly. "I hope he's all right."

"Mom, how could they? There's a big crew, and it sure would look funny if the nephew of the captain was the one to get the publicity."

"I don't see why," Maria's mother replied defensively. "Your brother is a Spaceman First Class now, and he's been on two expeditions to the Earth. Your uncle wouldn't take him if he wasn't needed. I'll bet Matthew has already made some wonderful scientific discoveries."

"That could be," the girl agreed. She read the short article again. "It doesn't sound to me as though there's any trouble. I don't see why you have to worry. After all, Uncle Lucky has flown to all sorts of nebulas and galaxies, and nothing's happened to him."

Her mother didn't answer at first. She poured canal juice into three glasses, smiling weakly. Finally she admitted, "Well, I reckon I wouldn't be Matthew's mother if I weren't really worried about him. Those flights out into space and everything—not like working in your father's powder factory, which is what I was hoping he'd do. Instead, *you're* going to work there, when I wanted you to be a famous actress."

"Gee whiz, Mom, the Moon has changed since you were a little girl. You can't expect a boy to get stuck in a powder factory these days, when so much is happening out there. I wouldn't mind taking a little space cruise myself."

Her mother almost dropped the pitcher. "Maria! Don't you dare talk like that! Imagine, both my children gallivanting around in the middle of nowhere, dodging meteors and wild asteroids." She began to sniffle. "And me sitting here alone all day wondering and worrying—"

"Goodness, Mom, don't take on so. I was only joking."

Mrs. Looney dabbed at her eyes, although there were no tears, for the lack of moisture on the Moon makes it practically impossible to

"I reckon I wouldn't be Matthew's mother if I weren't really worried about him."

carry on any really wet crying. She patted Maria's arm. "You're sweet. Now, set the table, like a good girl. Your father'll be here asking for food."

Monroe Looney, manager of the Mount Pico Powder Works, soon returned home. It had been a long day, and he was hungry. So after he had cleaned up, removing the dust from his clothes, hair and mustache, the family sat right down to dinner.

"Well, all set for tomorrow?" Mr. Looney asked, as he bit into one of those delicious, cave-made ash buns.

The two females cried excitedly that they were, and then began firing questions at him. "When do we leave?" "How long does it take?" "Can we see Matt or just hear his voice?"

"Wait a moonit, wait a moonit," Mr. Looney laughed. "Here's the plan. We take the early moonorail out of Crater Plato, right after breakfast, and we get off at Mooniversity Heights, on the outskirts of Crater Copernicus, the capital city of our happy sphere. I've got the tickets right here." He slapped his pockets and felt in first this one and then that. A look of alarm came over his face. "Where are they? Don't anyone leave the room! I've been robbed! Oh, here they are. Ahem."

"Really, Monroe," Mrs. Looney sighed. "You get me so nervous sometimes."

"Nothing to be nervous about, my dear. By the way, what's the weather report?"

"It'll be a nice, cold, clammy day, Monroe," Mrs. Looney told him. "The meteorites are supposed to hold off till Marsday."

"Good." The big fellow slapped both hands on the table. "Good. And now, Maria, I have something for you." He took a booklet out of his pocket and tossed it toward his daughter. She thumbed through it, while her father explained proudly, "That's the official history of the Mount Pico Powder Works, of which I am, as you well know, manager and part owner. As you will be starting your job there next month, I thought it a good idea for you to learn all about the plant." He leaned back and smiled. "You know? I was really disappointed when Matthew gave up that fine opportunity in the powder factory and chose to be a spaceman instead. But now I have Maria, here, and she's going to be the best little old powder gal you ever did see. Isn't she?"

"Well, I don't know, Daddy. I was wondering, must I go to work in the powder plant? It's so boring."

Mr. Looney's jaw dropped, and Mrs. Looney spoke sharply.

"Why, whatever makes you say such a thing? You ought to be proud that your father has given you a job there. The Mount Pico Powder Works is one of the most important businesses on the Moon. You know that the moonscape would be covered with piles of garbage and junk if we didn't have some way of grinding it up."

Maria pouted. "It's covered with piles already. We ought to live on Earth, where everything wears out and crumbles away all by itself. That's what Matt told me."

Her father laughed loudly. "Live on Earth? Where four-fifths of it is nothing but liquid? Where water falls from above when you least expect it? An Earth that spins and spins, never stopping? Oh, Maria, there are many reasons why you wouldn't live there, not the least of which is that the atmosphere is unhealthy. You'd soon choke on all that oxygen."

Maria stood up. "Well, there are plenty of other places in the Universe." She excused herself and left the room.

Mr. Looney called after her. "You're going to do your part in the family powder factory, young lady, and that's final!"

Back in her room Maria flopped on the bed in disgust. She glanced at the pamphlet for a moment and then threw it aside. From under her pillow she took out a sheet of paper with some printing on it, and studied it.

COSMIC COMFORT CORPS
Cave Box 40
Crater Copernicus

I hereby apply for the Cosmic Comfort Corps. I am willing to give my full time to the CCC. I realize that this may take me to the farthest reaches of the Universe. I want to help the downtrodden, hungry, lost inhabitants of other planets and galaxies.

Name ....
Address ....
Lunaphone ....
Job Preference 1
2
3

(If underage, parent's permission required.)
I give permission for my ——— to join the CCC.

Signed ———

At last she seemed to make up her mind, for she moved over to her desk, took up a graphite stylus and began to fill in the empty spaces that appeared on the page. Then she grasped the stylus firmly, and carefully wrote her father's name on the last line.

COSMIC COMFORT CORPS
Cave Box 40
Crater Copernicus

I hereby apply for the Cosmic Comfort Corps. I am willing to give my full time to the CCC. I realize that this may take me to the farthest reaches of the Universe. I want to help the downtrodden, hungry, lost inhabitants of other planets and galaxies.

Name ..... Maria Looney .....

Address .. 22 Zinc Rd. Crater .....

Lunaphone Plato 14 .... Plato

Job Preference ......
1 Child guidance
2 Librarian
3 Hydroculture

(If underage, parent's permission required.)
I give permission for my daughter to join the CCC.

Signed Monroe Looney

2. *Earth Strikes Again*

After breakfast the Looneys were packed and ready to go. In her room Maria had closed her nightcase and was holding the stamped, sealed envelope in her hand. Inside was the application.

I'll have to mail this some time when no one's watching.

Maria's heart thumped a little bit extra, as yours would too if you were asking to be sent anyplace in the Universe and, what's more, you had forged your father's name to the application. She stared at the envelope, planning what to do with it, when there was a loud clang, frightening the already nervous girl half out of her wits. Someone was knocking!

"Maria, are you ready? We've got to leave now." It was her mother, and the pitchstone door squeaked as she pushed it open. Maria barely had time to hide the envelope under the pillow. Mrs. Looney entered. "Are you all right, dear? You don't look pale."

"Yes, Mom, I'm okay."

"Well, come along or we'll miss the train."

Maria picked up her nightcase and followed her mother out. At the front entrance, Mr. Looney turned the key in the lock and gave it to Mrs. Looney. She placed it under the iron doormat. "There, that's for Lavinia. She's coming to clean the cave today."

The three started toward the station, carrying their bags. That wasn't difficult. As you know, gravity on the Moon is so weak that you just sort of ease along. If you're not careful, you might find yourself floating off the ground. Children are often stranded way up high when they play and jump. Once the Plato Low School was beaten in a championship craterball contest when their star player got overexcited and pushed himself up and away. He didn't come down until the game was over.

The moonorail was crowded, as a lot of Platoites were on their way to their offices in the capital. The Looneys found seats, and soon the train was speeding them up and over the rim and down the other side onto the Sea of Showers. The clear atmosphere of the lunascape was marred ahead by a tremendous cloud that came from the surface.

"Mount Pico!" called the conductor.

The moonorail slowed to a stop; Maria peered out the window.

"There's the powder factory," her father said proudly, pointing in the direction of the cloud. "See? There's a freight car filled with old furniture. We run that into the grinder, and out comes the powder. And over there is the moving belt that carries the powder off to the Alps, where it is used to fill up valleys and little craters."

Maria looked rueful. "Whatever could I do in a place like that?"

"Bookkeeping. We have to keep careful track of everything that goes in and comes out. Look! There's a truckload of old neckties. Oh, they make wonderful powder. Of course, they get tangled up in the grinders sometimes. But it's worth the effort. Do you know what they do on the Earth with them? They just keep on wearing them and using them. They don't have any fine factories like this to take care of the problem."

"That's right, Maria," her mother chimed in.

Maria was relieved when the moonorail started up again and Mount Pico disappeared in the distance. There were stops at Lambert and at Pytheas, little towns in the Sea of Showers where more commuters got on. Then the train plunged into a tunnel under the Carpathians, coming out on the other side, where the huge rim of Crater Copernicus loomed.

"Just think," said Mrs. Looney happily, "we'll soon be in touch with Matthew."

"Mooniversity Heights is the next station stop!"

The moonorail slid to a halt and the Looneys climbed out. Mr. Looney looked up and down the platform. "Where's Professor Ploozer? He said he'd meet us."

"Theodore P. Ploozer? The head of the whole space program? Is he going to meet us?" Maria asked in astonishment.

"Sure, why not?" her father replied. "We're old friends. He was in charge when Matt went to the Earth the first time. He's the chief high muckety-muck of the whole operation now, and he'll roll out the green gorgonzola for us, you'll see. There he is! Howdy, Prof! Here we be!"

Maria saw a long white beard approaching them. As it came closer she realized that there was a man attached to it, a man with no hair on top of his brown head, a man so short that she had to bend over to look into his eyes. But there was no green gorgonzola. Instead, the Professor started out by wailing and wringing his hands.

"Oh, my gegoodness, the Looney family! You received not my gemessage? I told you not to come. Maria, how you have gegrown, my dear! Didn't you hear the news? Hello, Mrs. Looney. It's top secret, how could you hear? Hello, Mr. Looney. It's gegood to see you. No, no, I mean it's not so gegood."

Mrs. Looney started sniffling. "Something's happened to my Matthew!"

"Now, now, Mrs. Looney, I'm sure everything will geturn out all right. Only a problem in communication, that's all. Just can't seem to focus the Interspatial Spectrophone where we want to. I mean, we gelost the *Feebey* but we gefound something else instead. Surprising."

"What are you trying to tell us, Professor?" asked Mr. Looney.

"Yes, yes, I am trying to getell you something, and this is it. On a routine inspection of the solar system, our Interspatial Spectrophone was — *what's that?*"

The Professor's voice was drowned out by a mighty howl. It was the meteorshower siren, warning everyone to find protection.

"There's a shower coming!" Maria cried.

"Come along, we can't getalk here," the Professor said. The four hurried away from the platform and down the road toward the Mooniversity.

"Didn't you gebring your parasols?" the scientist asked.

"The weather report was for cold and clammy," Mrs. Looney said in high dudgeon. "Wrong as usual."

There was a thumping noise and a chunk of meteorite struck near them.

"Oh, no, here they come," warned the Professor. "Here, getake my arm, Mrs. Looney."

Maria and her father hurried along behind the other two. "Why does he have that funny way of talking, Daddy?" she whispered.

"He's not a Moonster. He's from Ganymede, just outside Jupiter."

"I am trying to getell you something."

There was more and more thumping and the shower grew heavier. People were holding their obsidian parasols over their heads, and Maria heard the clink-clank of meteorites all around her. "Ouch!" she cried, as a particularly big piece landed on her shoulder. Up ahead there was a very high tower. Professor Ploozer steered them toward an entrance beneath the foot of it.

"Geduck in here." They hurried through an opening and into a large cave. As soon as they were out of danger, they relaxed.

"Made it," said Mr. Looney. "Where are we?"

"This is the Interspatial Spectrophone Building," Professor Ploozer explained. "That getower overhead sends and receives messages from the Universe. I was about to getell you, the most surprising—well, I'll geshow you. Gefollow me. We go the back way."

Shiny black halls stretched into the distance, lit by crystals that glowed brightly. Moonsters scurried back and forth carrying important papers, or stopping and whispering to each other about important matters. The bearded scientist led the Looneys through a door and up a short flight of steep, narrow stairs that soon led into one end of a large, brightly lighted room.

Against one wall were several comfortable armchairs where Professor Ploozer had the Looneys sit down. Spread out before them were machines and equipment, with wires, flashing lights, and—oh, all sorts of gadgets. Men in uniform twisted knobs, talked on visuaphones, wrote notes—it was so busy! But what stood out was the great big screen at the other end of the room.

"This is the gecenter of our Interspatial Spectrophone system," Professor Ploozer explained. "On that screen we can focus a gepicture of whatever galaxy, nebula, star, or planet we want to contact. Or we can reach the *Feebey* or any other ship out there. Or we can tie in with local Moon visuaphones."

"Amazing," breathed Mr. Looney.

"Are we going to talk to my Matthew on this machine?" the worried mother asked.

"Well, um, something has gehappened . . ." the Professor hesitated.

"Yes, Professor, please go on," Mr. Looney urged.

"Well, last night we were in geclose contact with the ship *Feebey*. She was cruising through the universe and all was well. When suddenly

—the *Feebey* disappeared! Gegone out of sight. More power, I asked for, but no good. The Interspatial Spectrophone searched and searched the heavens but could not gefind her."

"Oh, my poor boy! Lost in space!" Mrs. Looney was really upset. Mr. Looney and Maria tried to calm her.

"And then," the Professor went on, "while our big finders were gelooking for the *Feebey,* we picked up something else. Look!" He pointed at the giant screen, to which the Looneys in their confusion had not yet paid close attention. The picture was from somewhere out there, for the background was black and the lights of foreign bodies shone through. But taking up most of the scene was an odd object unlike anything from the Moon. There was a sharp nose on one end and what looked like rocket tubes at the other. Antennas and other fixtures stuck out here and there.

"What's that?" asked Mrs. Looney.

"That, my dear lady," said the Professor, "was a You-foe, an Unidentified Flying Object. Until a short getime ago. Now it's an Eye-foe."

"An Identified Flying Object?" Maria ventured shyly.

"What's that?" asked Mrs. Looney.

"Right, young gelady. And it is coming ge-closer and gecloser to the Moon. It will spy on us, or it will land. Without permission."

"Where is it from?" asked Mr. Looney.

"From Earth," said the Professor.

"From *Earth?* I thought we'd warned them to stop such invasions."

"We did. They paid no gattention. Not only that, but they have been carrying on like this while our Spatial Representative, Hector Horn-blower, is there trying to get those one hundred and four non-aggression treaties gesigned. Very poor interplanetary etiquette."

"I should say it is. What happens next?"

"The patience of the Moon is being sorely tried, sir," the scientist replied. "And this may well lead to solar hostilities."

"You mean—?"

"I gemean—*war!*"

"Oh, my," sniffled Mrs. Looney. "And my poor Matthew, out there in the middle of it."

"Now, now, madam," the bearded official as-sured her, "the *Feebey* is gefar away in a differ-ent part of the Universe. We just don't know where, that's all. I believe Admiral Looney will find his way home."

3. *The Horsehead Nebula*

"Right rudder four microsecs, Mr. Bones."

"Right rudder four microsecs," repeated the helmsman, changing course.

There was a growing tenseness on the bridge of the great ship *Feebey* as it sped through the vast wastes of the cosmos. So far the return voyage from Hercules had been without unusual incident, but now the first critical test approached. The commander, tall, white-haired Lockhard Looney, First Admiral in the Space Navy, appeared as confident as ever, as he glanced at the many instruments before him, or as he peered through the spaceshield to see what was ahead. But he and the others were aware that an unknown quantity lay there: they were about to plunge into the dreaded, mysterious Horsehead Nebula!

There was silence, except for the occasional murmur of the steering machine as it responded to Mr. Bones's movement of the wheel. The motors that drove the *Feebey* were idling, used only to speed up or slow down the vehicle, or to keep her from being captured by the gravity of some heavenly body. Otherwise, in the vacuum of space, no power was needed.

In his navigator's seat, Spaceman First Class Matthew Looney worked at the big, complicated astroputer that filled up a large part of the main deck.

"Give me a reading, Navigator!" came the Admiral's voice.

"Aye, aye, sir," replied Matt as he began making calculations with the information he had. He tapped the keys of the input unit, feeding figures to the instrument. Finally, he pushed a red button, there was a whirring noise, and the astroputer's tape came out, clickety-clack. Matt grabbed it and read the answer:

Beware the Ides of March.

"Hey, something's wrong," Matt muttered to

himself. He pushed the red button again. Another tape clicked its way out. It said:

Sticks and stones may break my bones
but names will never hurt me.

"Oh, you doggone stubborn machine," Matt said. "I'll show you who's boss." He went around to the side of the astroputer and kicked it. There was a clonk as his metal shoe struck home. Then came the familiar whirring and click as another tape emerged. Matt smiled triumphantly and grabbed it. He reported to Admiral Looney. "Diffusion dead ahead, sir. Eighty-eight lunacules distant as of—" he looked at his wrist parallax, "—now. We shall reach the area within twelve moonits."

"Very good." The great space explorer picked up the phone to the engine room. "Mr. Stottle, reverse engines. Mr. Bones, let me know when we are barely making way."

There was a muffled roar and the men were thrown forward as the *Feebey* put her brakes on. Soon Mr. Bones announced, "Now, sir."

"Stop engines!" Admiral Looney signaled the engine room. There was silence again. The big ship edged slowly through the starlit heavens. Admiral Looney looked through the spaceshield.

"Men, we are about to tackle the great unknown. There is the Horsehead Nebula, where no Moonster has gone before. Look."

Matt moved over to the front of the bridge where he could see better. Directly in front of them was a monstrous black cloud. It seemed to cover half the Universe, but Matt knew that was because they were so close. In all their voyages through the Universe, Matt and other moonflyers were able to see where they were going. No one had ever dared venture into the Horsehead Nebula for the good reason that it was not worth risking lives and spaceships. As the blackness came closer, Matthew wondered if it was worth it this time. He turned to his uncle.

"Sir?"

"Yes, Matt."

"Why are we going by this uncharted course? This isn't the way we came."

"It's a shortcut," the Admiral said quietly. "I haven't told the others, but we are desperately short of fuel. Believe me, boy, I wouldn't take this risk if we had enough to go the long way around."

"Entering Horsehead Nebula," said Mr. Bones.

"Man your navigator's post, Matt," said the Admiral.

Except for the occasional click of the meteor repeller, there was complete silence as the vessel was engulfed in the inky nothingness.

"Steady as she goes, Mr. Bones. What is our speed?" Admiral Looney looked through the spaceshield but he couldn't see anything. There was no reply from Mr. Bones and the commander sharply repeated his demand. "What is our speed?"

The mate's voice was strange. "Look! No speed! I don't know!"

The Admiral hurried to the instrument panel. The speed meter's wheels seemed to spin in all directions at once. In fact, every other dial and indicator was going crazy.

"Matt!" Admiral Looney snapped. "Give me a reading. I want our horizontal and vertical planes and a motion report. Quick!"

Matt tapped input keys and pushed the red activator button. The astroputer made not a sound. Matt tapped and pushed, turned and twisted, but he could get no response from the machine. He kicked it on all four sides, and finally there was a grunt as a short tape emerged.

"Look! No speed!"

Gone to lunch, it read. Matt turned to Admiral Looney with an alarmed look on his face. The wise commander immediately guessed the trouble.

"The Horsehead has put our instruments out of whack. Happened to me once in the Saturnine Rings. All right, Matt, try your monar."

Matt turned the big valve and waited for the tubes to warm up. He watched the monar screen but no picture appeared.

"Nothing, sir," he finally reported.

"I thought as much," Admiral Looney muttered. "We're flying blind. There's only one thing we can do now. Activate tactile scanner!"

Matt did as he was told. There was a shudder through the *Feebey* as the tactile scanner went into operation, stretching huge feelers out in front of the vessel. Matt sat in front of the big panel. The low murmur of the scanner began to get louder and louder, turning into a roar.

Matt tried to stay calm as he read the decibels.

"Large obstruction dead ahead!"

Admiral Looney grabbed the phone. "Mr. Stottle! Reverse engines!"

There was a jolt. "Stop engines!" Admiral Looney squinted at the spaceshield. "Oh, if I only knew whether we were moving up, down or sideways, front or backwards!"

"Uncle Lu—I mean, *sir!*" Matt was pointing out the side port next to his station. The blackness had changed to a reddish purple. A huge mass of some foreign body was right next to the ship. It passed slowly by the porthole, which meant that the *Feebey* still had some headway.

"Whew! Just missed that one," breathed Admiral Looney. "Keep that scanner going."

There was more roaring from the machine. "Another one coming up, sir!"

"Give me the wheel, Mr. Bones! Put out the starcatcher! Mr. Stottle, slow ahead! Matt, give me another scanner reading!" Admiral Looney's crisp orders rang through the bridge. His firmness and self-confidence kept the crew in good spirits. He carefully turned the wheel and sent the *Feebey* around another one of the purple masses that seemed to be everywhere in the nebula. Some of them were small enough to be thrust aside by the triangular starcatcher that projected from the nose of the vehicle. Now that there were these reference points, Matt and the others could tell that the *Feebey* was slowly creeping through the Horsehead Nebula. Ad-

"Whew! Just missed that one."

miral Looney used all the skills he had acquired from years of space travel, guiding the craft with his practiced hand.

"Well, I think we've got things under control now, men," their commander announced to the crew. "We've just safely passed not one, but two of the most dangerous obstacles in the Universe. The Horsehead Nebula and the Purple Pits of Polaris. I've often had nightmares of meeting up with one or the other—but never both at one time."

"I hope we never see them again, sir," Matt volunteered.

"Congratulations, Skipper," said the loyal mate.

"All in a day's work, Bones," the Admiral smiled. "I see a glimmer of starlight ahead. Here, take over. And Matt, raise Headquarters on your Spectrophone and we'll report in."

Matt went to his post, while the mate grabbed the wheel and steered the *Feebey* toward the welcome exit from the darkness of the nebula.

4. A Message from the Cosmos

SCENE: *Communications Room of Interspatial Spectrophone Building. Mr. and Mrs. Monroe Looney and daughter Maria are present. They have been there a long time, hoping for some word of their son, Matthew. None has come. They study the big ISP screen. Professor Ploozer is going back and forth from this instrument panel to that, from this technician to that. The screen still shows the strange-appearing Identified Flying Object from Earth. The speaker crackles.*

VOICE 1: IFO slowing down. Passing over Sea of Nectar.

PLOOZER: Which bearing?

VOICE 1: Two hundred forty. Closing fast.

PLOOZER: Plot her gelanding area.

VOICE 1: Roger. (*Pause.*) Crater Tycho.

MRS. LOONEY (*sniffles*): Whyn't they tune in on my boy Matthew?

MR. LOONEY: Hush, Mama. They're doing the best they can.

VOICE 2: Professor Ploozer. I'm getting signals from another quadrant. It's a space ship.

PLOOZER: Ask for gidentification.

VOICE 2: It's the *Feebey!* (*A quick cheer goes up among the men in the Communications Room.*)

MARIA: Oh, did you hear that, Mom?

PLOOZER: Put IFO on hold. Gebring in *Feebey.*

(*Picture on screen fades, and a new one forms. It is a face. It is Matthew Looney, Spaceman First Class. There are screams of joy from the Looneys.*)

MATTHEW: Hello, Moon. This is *S.S. Feebey.* Stand by for a message from Admiral Looney.

(*The Admiral's confident face appears.*)

ADMIRAL LOONEY: Ahem. This is your captain speaking. We are cruising at twelve hundred lunacules. Just off your stern you will note the Horsehead Nebula, and to your starboard you will find the giant red star Betelgeuse, which as you know is—

PLOOZER (*interrupting*): Admiral Gelooney! Admiral Gelooney! This is Moon Monitor calling. Stop telling us about the scenery. Why have you been gelost?

ADMIRAL: Oh, is that you, Ploozer? Gelost, my knuckle! Lockhard Looney is never gelost. You want to know where we've been—through the Horsehead, that's where.

PLOOZER (*impressed*): My gegoodness. That's why you disappeared from sight.

ADMIRAL: What's more, the Purple Pits of Polaris were floating around in there, too.

MR. LOONEY: The Purple *whats?*

MARIA: Quiet, please, Daddy.

PLOOZER (*more impressed*): My gegoodness! The Purple Pits. So that's where they've been. Are you damaged?

ADMIRAL (*chuckling*): No, no. We almost crashed into a couple of the big ones, but I was at the helm, so there was nothing to worry about. Of course, the crew helped, too.

MRS. LOONEY (*proudly*): See? That's my boy.

PLOOZER: Ah, that's the nuisance of flying through space. But we have also nuisance here at home.

ADMIRAL: What's that?

PLOOZER: Earth has gefired another missile our way, without warning.

ADMIRAL: What? After all the messages we've sent them about getting written permission? Is this one of the snoopers or one of the landers?

PLOOZER: It seems to be a gelander. There may be Earthers on board.

ADMIRAL: Why, the nerve of them! Say, I've got a loaded Lava-Three bomb with me. Why don't I let it fly at them?

PLOOZER: Now, now, Admiral. We can't do that.

ADMIRAL: Yes, yes, I know. But Earth has picked on our beloved Moon so much lately that I can't control myself. First they began sending those snoopers that went round and round, spying on us and then going back home. Then they sent missiles landing all over the place without any warning, once in a school yard, remember? Good thing no one was hurt.

PLOOZER: That's right.

ADMIRAL: We'll have to do something about this when I get back.

PLOOZER: Well, you are going to do something now. Here is a Spatial Delivery from Chairman R. T. Muss of Mongress.

ADMIRAL: Yeah? What's it say?

PLOOZER: It says: "Instruct Admiral Looney to make a report on living conditions in Hercules."

ADMIRAL: What for? Listen, Ploozer, that Cluster is a nice place to visit, but I'm not sure I'd want to live there. It's awful far from where the action is.

PLOOZER: It could be a military goutpost.

ADMIRAL: Might be useful as a base, at that. Okay, Professor, I'll add that to the report of my expedition. Now I'll turn you over to Spaceman Looney to sign off. (*Matt's face reappears.*)

MATTHEW: This is *S.S. Feebey* preparing to close this Interspatial Spectrophone channel.

PLOOZER: Just a gemoonit, Matt. Your folks are here.

MATTHEW (*brightening*): Oh, hi, Mom. Hi, Pop. I'll be home soon. Tell you all about Hercules when I see you.

LOONEYS (*all at once*): Hello, Matt. Oh, Matthew, are you all right? Good-bye, Matt.

PLOOZER: They wave and say hello, Matt. Sorry, cannot gopen up the channel for personal messages. You geknow how it is.

MATTHEW: Right, Prof. Thanks, and out. (*The picture fades.*)

MRS. LOONEY: Oh, thank you, Professor, for letting us stay and see our boy.

PLOOZER: Poof, it is nothing.

MR. LOONEY: Well, we really must be going. There's a long trip ahead of us back to Plato.

PLOOZER: Wait. Why not have a bite to eat in the gafeteria? Then come back here and I show you around.

MRS. LOONEY: Why, that's mighty neighborly. I think we'd be just delighted, wouldn't we, Monroe?

MR. LOONEY: Sure. (*Everyone leaves.*)

(*Later. Outside the door of the Communications Room the Looney family waits for Professor Ploozer.*)

MARIA: My, they have good food here, don't they? Those toasted limestones were good.

MRS. LOONEY: So was the murtle soup.

MR. LOONEY: Here, want a piece of volcandy?

MARIA: Thanks.

MRS. LOONEY: Wonder where the Professor could be? He said he'd meet us here.

(*The door bursts open and the Professor sticks his head out.*)

"Thank you for letting us stay and see our boy."

PLOOZER: Ah, there you are! Come in, come in! Most interesting gehappenings! A message from the IFO! (*He ushers the family back into the Communications Room.*)

MR. LOONEY: You mean there are Earthmen aboard her?

PLOOZER: Very poor signals, but someone tries to send messages. We don't know what their game is.

MRS. LOONEY: Oh, dear, it's such a nuisance. Now the Anti-Earthers will start their fussing again, wanting to blow up the planet.

MR. LOONEY: That would be going too far, but many of us think something must be done.

PLOOZER: Chairman R. T. Muss will make a State-of-the-Moon address on local lunavision. We pick it up on our Spectrophone. (*He gives instructions to an assistant. The big screen's wavy lines form into the face of the announcer.*)

ANNOUNCER: We interrupt our regular programs to bring you a special announcement. I speak to you from the caves of Mongress, where Mongressmen and other officials have heard the disturbing news that another missile from Earth is approaching, with passengers, and without warning. Chairman R. T. Muss will speak to the people about the situation. Chairman Muss.

(*The picture focuses on a new face.*)

CHAIRMAN MUSS: Fellow Moonsters, once again our territory is being violated by Earth. Snoopers and landers have been pestering us for a long time, flying aimlessly through our space or coming down on private property without permission and almost causing injuries on some occasions. Now we hear from our Space Headquarters that this latest missile has some Earthers on it. We will be happy to hear what message they bring. As you know, Spatial Representative Hector Hornblower has been on Earth for some time now, trying to get the many different tribes there to sign a treaty which would guarantee our boundaries. So far, no word has come from him. Now, I am taking two steps. I am asking Mongress to hold hearings to decide what to do. And I shall lead a welcoming party to Crater Tycho, where the Earth missile will land. In the meantime, I appeal to you all to be calm, and especially to the Anti-Earthers, who this very moonit are picketing and agitating right here in the capital, again demanding that the Earth be destroyed as a solution to the matter. As long as I am Chairman, I will not agree to such extreme action. Now, let us all join in singing our lunar anthem. (*Music is heard and the Looneys join in along with the others in the room.*)

"Oh, beautiful, for space's eyes,
Above the pock-marked plain,
In purple-cratered majesty,
Your dusty mountains reign.
Oh, Moon of mine, oh, Moon of mine,
I praise your darkened sphere,
And hope that light will ever shine
On you from year to year."

(*The picture fades. The Looneys are silent a moment, then prepare to leave for home, bidding farewell to Professor Ploozer. They catch the moonorail at Mooniversity Heights and after an uneventful trip find themselves back in their cave in Zinc Street, Plato. Maria goes to her room to rest. She is delighted to find it all cleaned up, with fresh sheets on the bed.*)

MARIA (*to herself*): My, I'm glad I didn't send

"Oh beautiful, for space's eyes . . ."

in that application for the Cosmic Comfort Corps. I wouldn't want to be out there in the Universe when it's so unsettled. Besides, all the action is really here on the Moon. And I shouldn't have signed Daddy's name. That wasn't right. I'll tear it up.

(*She is about to stick her hand under the pillow when she sees a note on the bed.*)

dere Maria
Maled yur
Letter fer
ya.
Lavinia

5. *Arrivals from Earth*

Tycho is a wilderness. It is surrounded by other rugged craters such as Wilhelm the First, Saussure, Maginus, and the huge Clavius. It is a part of the Moon that Moonsters seldom visit. Those who do go at their own risk. The giant Hipparchus roams freely, and will swallow whole any moving thing. At the other extreme, there are bullions and bullions of tiny, tiny vogels. They are harmless, except when there is a loud noise. Frightened, a band of vogels rushes together, forming a tremendous ball which rolls up and down slopes, crushing whatever is in its path.

If you will glance at your map, you will see

that to go from Copernicus to Tycho in a straight line, you must cross the Sea of Clouds. This is almost never successful, for you just cannot find your way through the mists. The sensible route is to take the Lunar Transit that goes to the Sea of Tranquillity, but get off at Marco Polo, turn right, and just start walking. (There is no fancy moonorail in that part of the sphere.) Now, Moonsters are very curious, and despite the inconvenience, many of them decided to go to Tycho to see the latest missile from Earth. They straggled along the route, kicking up a lot of dust, and laughing or arguing or doing whatever they could do to entertain or busy themselves.

One of the groups that was better organized than the others was the Anti-Earth League. Robinson K. Russo, a very important Moonster, was the head of the League and he was marching toward Tycho with many of its members. The League had one goal: to get rid of Earth. They were always picketing, writing, making speeches, trying to get Mongress to pass a law against Earth, to declare it illegal, and to abolish it. Now that Earth had struck again, the League picked up more joiners.

That's what happened each time another space shot came from Earth: more and more Moonsters decided that the Earth must be put out of the way. At each election, more Mongressmen were elected who campaigned on an Anti-Earth platform. Bills to blast the Earth were brought up all the time and defeated, but the vote got closer and closer. Moonsters were usually divided into two groups: the blasters, who said to drop the bomb and let 'em have it; and the softies, who said it would take innocent lives and would be unfair. (The bomb was the newfangled Lava-Four, a terrifying space weapon.) The blasters claimed that if the Earthers weren't stopped now, they would become stronger and would take over the Moon. The softies believed that all spacefolk could live happily together.

Of course, it was hard to explain why all sorts of strange devices were continually plopping down and around the Moon, landing in gardens and on cavetops without warning, scaring a person half to death, or circling the Moon a few times and then moving away, like a spy. It was very suspicious. If Earthers were friendly, why not approach through diplomatic channels? Why not sign the treaties carried by Spatial

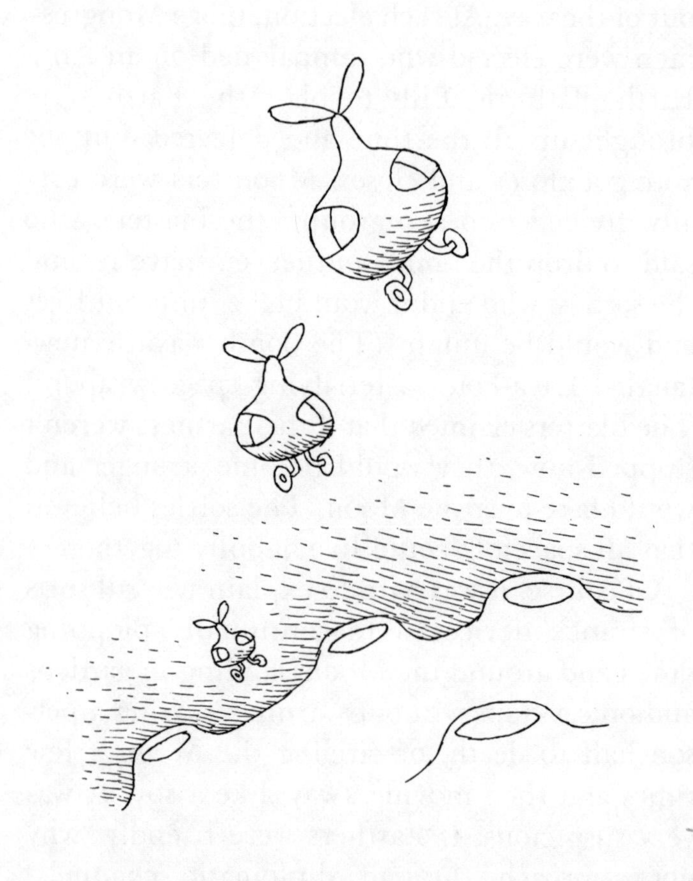

The molacopters disappeared in the distance.

Representative Hornblower? That was the mood of the Moon—puzzled and angry—as this new intrusion was due. And a lot of the Moonsters who hit the road for Tycho were hoping that this time the matter could be settled somehow, one way or another.

Robinson K. Russo's followers were skirting the edge of Crater Arzachel, more than halfway to their destination, when a humming sound in the distance grew and grew. All looked up to see many molacopters flapping by overhead.

"There they go," muttered Russo. "Those are the big shots. They ride while we walk."

In the molacopters were the government officials and other VIP's: R. T. Muss, Chairman of the Moon; Professor Ploozer and his scientists; members of the Mongressional Committee on Cosmic Affairs; and reporters for lunavision and the mewspapers. The molacopters disappeared in the distance and the marchers kept going. When they came to the heights of Regiomontanus, there were two ways to go: the high road and the low road. Robinson K. Russo looked at his map and his *Moonguide*.

"*When approaching Regiomontanus,*" he read aloud from the *Moonguide*, "*the trav-*

eler must beware the foothills where the giant Hipparchus lives."

"Okay, let's take the high road!" someone shouted.

" . . . *and if one goes through the highlands,*" Russo continued, "*it is necessary to keep absolute silence or else the bands of vogels will start rolling.*"

Everyone was very quiet, looking around fearfully.

"There is only one answer," said Russo, "and that is to take the middle road."

They moved softly and without a sound across the slopes of Regiomontanus, between Ball and Lexell, finally coming upon the walls of Tycho in the distance, and reaching that crater without mishap.

The scene was one of great confusion. There were crowds of Moonsters milling about. There were all the officials. And there were a number of vendors hawking their wares.

"Get your space balloons here, folks."

"Cold canal juice! Ten rubbles a glass."

"Programs! Can't tell the flyers without a program!"

Tycho used to be a mining village, and some

old caves had been cleaned up and made into quarters for the officials. The floor of the crater was clear, and it was there that the IFO from Earth would land. Professor Ploozer and his assistants had put up a portable azimuthal alidade and were aiming it toward Earth, trying to pick up the incoming space vehicle. Pretty soon they spotted it.

"Here she comes!" yelled the man operating the alidade. "And she'll land right here!"

"Ah," smiled the Professor. "Just as I guessed."

R. T. Muss and the others waited. They could not see the ship yet. They stood on a green gorgonzola which had been laid out for the arriving Earthman or Earthmen, as the case might be. A platoon of Royal Moonties were on hand to keep order. Then the ship came into view. She was a big white object approaching at great speed. Suddenly there was a roar and she spat out long, red flames from her rockets. She turned around and backed slowly toward the crater. Closer and closer she came until the rockets gently let her down onto the bumpy surface of the Moon. When she touched, the rockets shut off and there was silence.

R. T. Muss, Professor Ploozer, and those closest started toward the strange vehicle. It thrust three long legs out, setting feet on the ground to keep the ship steady. A ladder slowly dropped down from the ship, and at the top of the ladder could be seen a hatch with a window in it. There was some movement behind the window. There really was some living thing on board the spaceship! The crowd gathered closer, wondering. The Moonties pushed everyone back and made room around the ship. The big wheel on the outside of the hatch turned, and turned, and turned. Would it never open? Finally there was a screech, and the door was pushed outward. A face appeared. It was not an Earth face. It was a Moon face. Professor Ploozer recognized it immediately.

"Hector Hornblower!" he exclaimed.

Chairman Muss looked surprised. "Our Spatial Ambassador? Are you sure?"

"Certainly I'm sure. He was a gestudent in my space class. Matthew Looney, too. Before they made those trips to Earth."

They went to the ladder and waited for Hornblower to descend. Reporters and cameramen jostled them. The fat little fellow came halfway

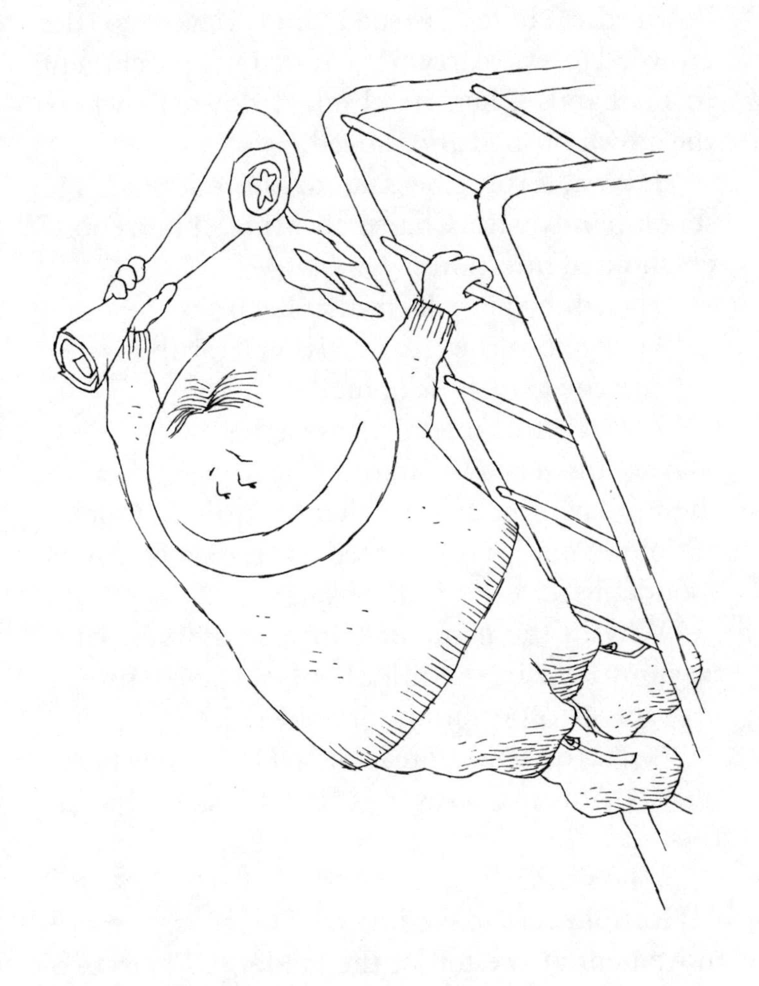

The fat little fellow waved at the crowd.

down the ladder, turned, and waved to the crowd. He was carrying a rolled-up parchment in his hand. Then he climbed down to where the crowd pushed and shoved.

"Hi, ya, Prof," he said to the scientist. He shook hands with Chairman Muss. The reporters shouted questions.

"Hey, did you really fly that heap?"

"How about the treaty, Mister Hornblower?"

"Are you glad to be home?"

"Look at the camera, please, fella."

Any answers Hornblower gave were lost in the uproar. Finally he called for quiet. "One at a time. You." He pointed at the lady correspondent from the *Daily Planet*.

"Why in the name of Universe did you land way out here in the middle of nowhere instead of at the spaceport in the Sea of Crisis?"

"Good question, ma'am," Hornblower replied. "And the answer is that I wasn't drivin' the thing."

"Who was?"

Hornblower looked up. There was more movement at the top of the ladder. "Them two fellas."

Everyone's attention was suddenly on the hatch

of the spaceship. Someone else was aboard. Two figures appeared and started down the ladder. They were Earthmen! They were wearing tanks of breathing gas because, as Moonsters know, Earthmen cannot live on the Moon without it. They also wore heavy weights to help the weak gravity hold them on the ground. The crowd's mood changed and they booed. The Royal Moonties held them back. As the strangers stepped off the ladder, Ambassador Hornblower introduced them.

The short fat one was Dr. Leonard O. Davinchy. The tall one with the big nose was Wiley Kalmuck. Professor Ploozer recognized them as the two who had visited the Moon once before.*

"Why, how do you gedo, friends," he said. (Moonsters are able to speak and understand any language in the Universe, as far as we know.)

"Ah, Ploozer," smiled the short Dr. Davinchy.

"Oh, it's you again, eh?" grouched the skinny Kalmuck. Ploozer remembered him as a sorehead and troublemaker. The Earthmen were introduced to Chairman R. T. Muss. All the

* The story of that voyage, and of Hector Hornblower's departure for Earth, is told in *Matthew Looney's Invasion of the Earth*.

while the mewspapermen were shouting questions. The Anti-Earth Leaguers had set up a terrific booing and hissing. Matters were getting out of hand, so the Royal Moonties forced a path through the shouting crowd and led the newcomers and the welcoming party across the crater floor to one of the fancy caves that had been furnished for officials. The door was clanged shut and the cries of the hecklers could barely be heard.

"This is better," said Chairman Muss. "It is a genuine pleasure to welcome you to our Moon, gentlemen. Ambassador Hornblower, if you will conduct our guests into my office, we shall get on with the business of the day."

"One moment, please!" A man in a green uniform stepped up to the two Earthmen. "May I see your passports?" He held out his hand.

"It's the Customs Inspector," someone remarked.

Wiley Kalmuck's pink face grew pinker, and he snarled, "Passports? Is this some kind of joke, Buster?"

But Dr. Davinchy calmed his companion. "It's all right, Wiley. He wants some identification. How about a driver's license?" The Cus-

"It's the Customs Inspector."

toms Inspector nodded, and the two men got out their wallets and found the proper papers.

"All right," the Inspector ordered. "Open your baggage."

"*What?*" Kalmuck cried. "I'll open your head if you—"

"Wiley, please!" Dr. Davinchy said sharply. To the Inspector he added, "We have no baggage with us."

The Inspector looked suspicious and got a pencil and paper out. "Any fruit? How long will you stay? Do you expect to earn any money while here?" Etc. etc. The questions went on and the men answered as best they could. Finally the Inspector folded the paper and stepped back. "Now take off your shoes. I'll give you your shots." He took up a tremendous pointed gun and aimed it. The men cringed.

Chairman Muss explained. "It's for moononucleosis."

The men each removed a shoe and the Inspector fired the gun into the big toe. "Ouch!" they both cried.

The inspection over, they went into the Chairman's office and sat down. R. T. Muss smiled happily at Hector.

"We are glad to have you return to Moon, Mr. Ambassador. I see you carry the treaties with you, all signed, sealed, and delivered, I imagine. This means that we shall not be bothered with unauthorized visits from Earth any more."

Hector Hornblower stood in front of the Chairman. He spread out the treaties on the desk. He didn't look pleased as he replied.

"Mr. Chairman, I am sorry to hafta report that it ain't as rosy a pitcher as you think. When I went to Earth I had a hundred and four blank treaties. I went to a place called the United Tribes and tried to get 'em signed. While I was waitin', eighteen more tribes joined up. That put me short eighteen copies."

"Well, if you got one hundred and four signatures, that's excellent. We can get the rest later."

"But I didn't."

"How many tribes did agree not to land on the Moon without permission?"

"Two. Albanians and Japanese. The others refused. Some of them were real nasty."

Chairman Muss stood up in alarm. Other minor officials in the room gasped in disbelief.

Hornblower shook his head and shrugged his shoulders.

"I tried," he remarked sadly.

Then Wiley Kalmuck jumped up. "Look, I don't know what this is all about. We're certainly not signing any treaty. I don't know if you ever heard of the United States. That's where I come from. We wouldn't be where we are today if we went around signing treaties like that. Now we're here on the Moon and we aim to stay. Any of you punks that try to stop us—we'll make mincemeat out of you. Come on, Davinchy, we got work to do."

He turned and stalked out of the cave. Everyone was shocked into silence. Then Chairman Muss mumbled, "What is mincemeat?"

6. The Conquest

The lunar situation was very, very tense. In the caves around Crater Tycho, a temporary government had been established. Chairman Muss ran the Moon's business from there. The Mongressional Committee on Cosmic Affairs started an investigation. Ambassador Hector Hornblower was the first to testify. He told the whole story of how no one on Earth would pay any attention to him, and in some cases threw him in jail and in others just wouldn't even talk to him.

"They're mean cusses, them Earthers," he declared.

Robinson K. Russo came before the Committee, too. He reported that the Anti-Earth League had more members than ever before, and that they all were voters. He warned that Earth was planning to take over the Moon, and that the only way to stop it was to strike first.

"We have the Lava-Fours available," he frowned. "A couple of them laid onto that miserable, spinning, lopsided hunk of iron would let us live in peace once more." He banged the table and shouted, "There have been a hundred incidents so far! How many more before you people wake up!"

The hearings went on, while out on the floor of the crater there was more activity. A lot of Moonsters, most of them followers of Robinson K. Russo, were hanging around just to see what would happen. They lived in the abandoned caves and ate food that some smart operators carried overland and sold at very high prices. The Earthship, which everyone found out was called *Apollo,* was guarded by the Royal Moonties. Dr. Davinchy and Wiley Kalmuck lived aboard, but came out often. As Moonsters are essentially harmless, the Earthmen were quite safe. Professor Ploozer and Dr. Davinchy, scientists at heart, exchanged all sorts of information and were becoming great friends. Kalmuck, however, was actually a member of the secret service, and one of his jobs was to spy on the Moon, but no one knew that.

The lanky Earthman was invited to appear before the Cosmic Affairs Committee. Chairman Muss was presiding. He started by saying, "We are trying to get at the bottom of things. We would like to ask you a few questions."

Kalmuck settled back in his chair. "Shoot."

"As you may know from your study of the history of space, the Moon is open to all. Visitors come and go, and some stay to live here. All we ask them to do is to obey our laws. Now, if you unfortunate Earth-dwellers wish to move to our more bountiful Moon, we are happy to have you. However, we insist that you stop bombarding our towns and our public lands with your missiles."

"Look, fella, our *Apollo* came down nice and easy without hurting a soul, didn't it?"

"Yes, Mr. Kalmuck, it did. But it was the first time. In the past we have had to dodge all sorts of contraptions that suddenly plop down from the sky. And others of them just fly around and around, never landing, and that makes us very nervous. We just cannot go on like this. That's why we have tried to get the Earth to sign these nonaggression treaties. It's for your own good."

"For our own good?"

"Certainly. A large number of Moonsters wish to destroy the Earth. It would be a good idea for you to play ball."

"Look, Buster, I can't speak for the others, but the United States will never sign. If there is any destroying to be done, we'll do it."

"You're a very stubborn fellow to convince, Mr. Kalmuck. I might point out to you that the Moon has never lost a war yet."

"Oh, really? Who have you beaten?"

"Well, we have never won a war, either, because we have never fought one," Chairman Muss went on. "And we do not intend to start now."

"That's ridiculous," Kalmuck snickered. "How are you going to conquer space if you don't fight it out? How do you defend yourself from enemies?"

"There is really no need to conquer space, as you put it. Space is there, that's all. As for defending ourselves, it's very simple. We show our potential enemy the power of our weapons, and each time they are always happy to declare peace."

Kalmuck chuckled. "Weapons? Weapons? Why, you people don't even have gas stations or Coke machines. How could you have any weapons worth looking at?"

"They all ask the same question, Mr. Kalmuck," R. T. Muss replied. "When the time comes for our demonstration, you will get your answer. Now, let's get on with the hearings."

The Mongressional Committee on Cosmic Affairs listened to many witnesses with different ideas on what to do about the threat from Earth. However, there were at least two Moonsters who did not appear, and they were among the most important ones: Admiral Lockhard Looney and Spaceman Matthew Looney. They had been to Earth twice; they had flown elsewhere in the Universe; their opinions were needed. But the *Feebey* was still speeding homeward, and would not land at the Space Expeditionary Forces spaceport in the Sea of Crisis for a while yet. While the Committee was waiting for their arrival, Chairman Muss and Mongress decided to have a Lava-Four Bomb fired into space as a public warning to Earth.

"Oh, boy, I can just see the Earth shriveling up."

The Moon Space Navy had only two Lava-Four bombs in its arsenal back at the Sea of Crisis. There were Lava-Ones, Twos, and Threes, but just two Fours had been made. On orders from Chairman Muss, one of these, with its launching platform, was flown by big freight molacopters to Crater Tycho, where it was set up not far from the Earthship. It was the first look for most Moonsters, and they crowded around. The front end was the business end—in it was a charge of helio-activated compressed lava. The trigger was a core of flint. The exact working of the Lava-Four was secret, and you couldn't understand it even if it were not. But the general idea was that the flint would set the lava on fire, and it would expand, flowing all over the target, melting it and suffocating it. There were delicate steering devices to make sure the bomb landed where it was supposed to. The Lava-Four was made for big, round, watery targets like the Earth.

Robinson K. Russo went up to the shiny thing and patted it. "Oh, boy, I can just see the Earth shriveling up into nothing."

Dr. Davinchy and Kalmuck were curious. They walked around and around the weapon.

"What do you think, Wiley?" asked Dr. Davinchy, looking puzzled.

"Crazy, man, crazy. It'll never work."

Just then a number of members of Mongress came up, with Chairman Muss at their head. He carried a galactic chart and pointed to a spot on it.

"Gentlemen, right here is our target, the uninhabited star Eta Ursae Majoris. Our Lava-Four will remove it from the Universe, turning it into gas. We shall make a sight and sound record of the event and you will be expected to show it to your leaders, who may then stop threatening us and disobeying our tourist regulations and other laws. When they see what one of our bombs can do, they may even want to sign a treaty."

Dr. Davinchy was scratching his head in puzzlement. Wiley Kalmuck was smirking. He laughed, "Okay, Chairman, go right ahead."

The instruments were adjusted, and the Lava-Four was aimed toward the blackness of the sky. Tiny and distant Eta Ursae Majoris could barely be seen from Tycho, so the automatic finder had to be tuned in. Except for the technician who would fire the bomb, everyone else was standing back to be safe. Finally he hurried away from the launching site and joined the others. There was a grinding noise from the Lava-Four.

"It's the countdown," the technician said. About one minute later he added, "There she goes."

With a roar, smoke spurted out, and the bomb quickly shot off into the sky. Her red rockets pushed her steadily up, up and away until only the smoke and smell were left.

"Takes off in a hurry, all right," said Kalmuck.

"Weak gravity, lack of air resistance, and so forth," Dr. Davinchy pointed out to his colleague.

"Yeah? Well, it's a phony, that's for sure. You don't believe that baloney about melting a star, do you?"

"It's highly unlikely, Wiley. Let's just see what they do next."

"Well, I know what I'm going to do next."

"What do you mean?"

"What I mean, Doc, is—" Kalmuck lowered his voice "—I was sent here with special orders that I didn't even reveal to you. When the time

"This is an astroputer connected with an interspatial spectrophone."

is ripe, and it looks ripe right now, I am supposed to—oh-oh, here they come. I'll tell you later."

Chairman Muss, Professor Ploozer, and some officials approached the Earthmen. "Ah, gentlemen," the Professor beamed, "you must be impressed by our weapon. Now, over here we have another ginteresting machine." He led the men to a complicated apparatus which had been installed on the edge of the crater floor. "This is an astroputer connected with an Interspatial Spectrophone. It will track the Lava-Four and make a record of what happens to our target."

"And then," Chairman Muss smiled, "Earth, and even your Untied Stakes, will be most happy to cooperate."

"United States," Kalmuck corrected him. "How long do we have to wait for this?"

"Oh, it will be a day or getwo," Ploozer said. "Come, Davinchy, you and I have some work to finish."

The Professor grabbed the Earthman's arm. Dr. Davinchy held back. "Wait, I want to talk to Wiley. He was telling me—" But Kalmuck was already well on the way to the *Apollo* spaceship, and with Ploozer tugging at him, Dr.

Davinchy had to leave without learning what the special orders from Earth were.

He soon found out.

Chairman Muss and members of Mongress were in their cave headquarters. Ploozer and Davinchy were in the temporary cave laboratory. In the communications cave, scientists were busy observing all lunar and spatial activities of importance—such as the path of the returning *Feebey* and the track of the outgoing Lava-Four. Suddenly one of the men called for attention.

"The *Apollo* is sending!"

The other communications men dropped their tasks for the time being. Someone called Chairman Muss and the others. Ploozer and Davinchy appeared.

"It's a message to Earth," the communications man said. He listened some more through his headphone, and then he switched to the speakers. Wiley Kalmuck's voice boomed out: ". . . would report first chance. Here goes. Have landed safely, without mishap. Crater Tycho as planned. Smooth landing area. No opposition. Moonsters act like magicians more than anything. Shot some firebomb into space to scare Davinchy and me. Didn't fall for it. Looks like it's a cinch. Will activate Operation Conquistador immediately. Roger and out."

With that Kalmuck signed off.

Chairman Muss looked at Dr. Davinchy. "What does it mean?—*konk—keesta*—never heard that word before."

"Conquistador," Davinchy said quietly. "I have an idea what it means. Hmm." He went to the entrance to the cave and looked out toward the *Apollo*. The others followed. They saw Wiley emerge from the ship.

"What's he doing?" Chairman Muss asked. "He's carrying a long stick with a rag on one end. It's a rag with white and red stripes on it. There's a blue square with white spots on it. He's sticking it into the ground. It must be a religious custom. He's standing in front of it. He's pointing his fingers at his forehead. What's the meaning of this, Davinchy?"

Without answering, the Earthman started across the broad, flat area. The Moonsters were right along with him. When they got to Kalmuck, he faced them all and shouted:

"I hereby claim this area in the name of the United States of America! You are now on Federal property! And as for this here place, I christen thee Crater Kalmuck!"

Dr. Davinchy grabbed his partner by the arm. "For heaven's sake, Wiley, you can't plant the flag here. You're not Cortes in Mexico. This is the twentieth century. The Moon belongs to everyone. The best things in life are free."

Kalmuck grinned. "Come on, Doc, take it easy. Play your cards right, and I'll name something after you. 'Crater Davinchy.' Sounds pretty good, eh? Ho, ho, ho." He laughed gleefully.

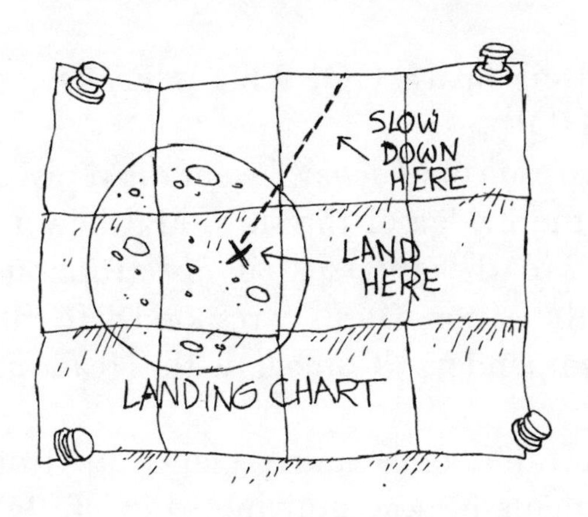

7. Tragedy at Tycho

About one hundred minicules from that American flag was the large, flat Sea of Crisis, where Space Expeditionary Forces had its headquarters and a landing field for vehicles that journeyed into the cosmos. The technicians and scientists there paid little attention to what was happening far away at Tycho, because they were busy getting ready for the arrival of the great ship *Feebey,* returning from her exploration of the distant Hercules Globular Cluster. At about the same time that Wiley Kalmuck was carrying out his secret orders at Tycho, a message crackled over the Interspatial Spectrophone at the Sea of Crisis:

"Calling Space HQ! This is *Feebey*, calling Space HQ!"

"We read you, *Feebey*," went the reply.

On the bridge of the ship, Matthew Looney sat before the Interspatial Spectrophone and heard the Moon Monitor respond. He called to his commander. "Contact with Headquarters, sir."

Admiral Looney didn't glance up from the instruments he was studying so carefully. "Request landing instructions."

Matt relayed this message to the Moon, and soon the answer was forthcoming. "HQ to *Feebey*. Olivium Runway cleared for your approach. Inclination of orbital plane to ecliptic, five degrees, fourteen moonits. Meteor showers in vicinity of Alhazen. Suggest you come in via Macrobius. Over."

Matt plotted the instructions on his chart and passed it to Admiral Looney, who affixed the chart to the panel before him. He had taken the wheel from his loyal helmsman, Mr. Bones, as the landing of the big ship, low on fuel, was a delicate task.

"Diurnal libration, Mr. Looney."

Matt quickly shot back the information.

"Plus or minus fifty-seven on the parallactic, sir."

The Admiral turned the wheel one midgeon.

"Watch the monar for Macrobius."

"Aye, aye, sir."

Matt's eyes moved back and forth across the astroputer's board, its many-colored lights and clicking tape telling him the whole story of the *Feebey*'s descent. He wrote with his stylus on the flight sheet.

"Macrobius off the starboard beam," he finally called.

Admiral Looney swung the wheel and the big vessel gently changed direction.

"Orbital plane six degrees, sir."

The Admiral started to level off. He picked up the intercom. "Mr. Stottle! Ready with engines."

The *Feebey* glided silently along. Now the crew could look through the spaceshield and see where they were headed. The broad expanse of the Sea of Crisis lay below. Matt stole a peek at the welcome sight, then went back to his duties.

"Reverse engines!" the Admiral ordered. Unlike the primitive Earthship, *Apollo,* the big, modern *Feebey* did not have to turn around and back in to a landing. It wasn't long before she had settled safely on the ground, and the cheers of the crew echoed throughout. Admiral Looney pushed open the main hatch and led his men onto the cold, friendly home soil. They breathed deeply the delightful vacuum of their beloved Moon. Then they looked around in puzzlement.

There was no one there to greet them.

No reporters, no cheering crowds, no important officials. All the movement to be seen was a land craft coming toward them from the edge of the Sea, where the Space HQ caves were situated. But when it reached them, the disappointed spacemen saw that it contained only a few mechanics who were going to clean up the *Feebey,* refuel her, and move her into the hangar. Matt spoke to one of them.

"Where is everybody, Corporal?"

The young Moonster shrugged. "All over at Tycho, I guess. That's where the action is."

"What action?"

"Haven't you heard? Some Earthers landed. They want the Moon for themselves. First come, first served, they said. Don't you read the papers? Everybody's talking about it."

"We've been away, young man," Admiral Looney muttered sarcastically. "Matt, get on the lunaphone and raise Professor Ploozer. Find out what this is all about."

Matt hurried back into the *Feebey*'s main cabin, while the others stood about and speculated on the rumor. In a few moments he hurried back. "It's true! Two travelers from that antique planet have claimed Crater Tycho for their leaders, and perhaps will try to conquer the entire Moon!"

"Whom did you talk to?"

"Chairman Muss, mostly. He wants a report immediately on Hercules."

Admiral Looney shook his head. "That's out of the question. We've got a lot of work to do here before we can close out this expedition. Hmm. Listen, Matt, you'll just have to go there by yourself and make that report for all of us."

So it happened that Matt found himself flying by molacopter across the wastes of the Sea of Tranquillity, down the valley of Abulfeda, and into the crater called Tycho (except by Kalmuck, the Earthman). There, in contrast to the reception at Crisis, he was greeted warmly. His old friend, Professor Ploozer, and his chief of state, Chairman Muss, and many other friends and acquaintances made him welcome and plied him with many questions about his recent adventure in space.

Matt, of course, had a few questions of his own. He was told about the arrival of the *Apollo,* of the Operation Conquistador by the newcomers, of the firing of the Lava-Four, and other events. To his surprise he found that the two Earthmen were the same two whom he had met when he had made his second journey to the ugly planet some time before.

Very shortly after Matt reached Crater Tycho, the Mongressional Committee on Cosmic Affairs went into session for the purpose of hearing the long-awaited report on Hercules. The expedition had gone there merely to explore. Now its discoveries were of more than just scientific interest. Matt was prepared, with the *Feebey*'s log, with cosmographs that had been taken there, and with a diary he had kept. After telling something of the trip there, Matt then described the galaxy.

"As you know, gentlemen, Hercules lies in the area of Sagittarius. It is a great globular cluster of many stars, most of them jammed into

"As you know gentlemen, Hercules lies in the area of Sagittarius."

the center. We flew from one to the other, gathering information. Most of them were too hot or too cold to be of any value, but we found one that contained a planetary system. That is the white star Freeholy, and around it circled a dozen satellites, any one of which would be a fine spot for a vacation. Two of these, which we have named Enchilada and Tamale, are pretty little places with good weather and no meteorite showers."

"Spaceman Looney," Chairman Muss asked, "were there any inhabitants on these heavenly bodies?"

"None that we could see."

"Can you tell us more of the living conditions there?"

"Certainly," Matt went on. "The two planets seem to be composed of mixtures of clastic and nonclastic rock. Without meteor showers, there would be no need for cave dwellings, and buildings could be made of this rock. The vacuum is suitable for breathing, especially on Tamale, while on Enchilada there are ribbons of moving water, which would provide a way for settlers to dispose of trash. And there is a food supply."

Committee members asked many more questions of Matthew regarding the newly discovered planets. The meeting was adjourned finally, while the committee went into private session, giving Matt a chance to relax almost for the first time since his return to the Moon. Although he had gotten in touch briefly with his family in Crater Plato when he first landed, to tell them of his safe arrival, it was only now that he had the time for a chat over the long-distance lunaphone. He promised that he would be home as soon as he was released from active duty.

Then Matt wandered about the Crater, mingling with the Moonsters who were camping out in the uninhabited caves, watching and waiting to see what was going to happen. Would the Moon be invaded by Earth? What would Mongress decide to do about this latest in the long series of illegal landings? Matt talked with Dr. Davinchy and Kalmuck and visited the *Apollo*. He told them of his trip to Hercules, although Wiley Kalmuck, true to form, didn't believe a word of it. Matt then stopped off at the portable astroputer that was tracking the Lava-Four, still on its way to Eta Ursae Majoris. According to the reading, the weapon had a ways

Matt climbed into his sleeping bag.

to go yet before reaching its target and turning it into gas. *When the Earth sees what we can do,* Matt reflected, *she'll leave us alone forever and ever.*

After eating a lavaburger and washing it down with canal juice—a meal that his mother would not have approved of—Matt was about ready to collapse from exhaustion. He had not had a real rest for a long time, so he unrolled his sleeping bag in a mini-crater on the edge of Tycho, climbed in, and dropped off to sleep. If he dreamed, they were dreams of faraway celestial places, and not of the turmoil and excitement that was going on nearby. He didn't know how long he had been sleeping, when he was awakened by a thumping and roaring. It took a few moments for him to realize where he was and what was taking place, but finally he got himself oriented. He stood up and looked in the direction of the *Apollo.* A tremendous mob of Moonsters were circling the big ship. Their marching feet shook the ground, and their shouts and jeers rattled his head uncomfortably. He went toward the scene and saw that Robinson K. Russo and his Anti-Earth Leaguers were on the move again. They stomped around the flag that Wiley Kalmuck had planted, and then they snaked around the *Apollo* itself. They carried signs that told their viewpoint:

BEAUTIFY THE UNIVERSE—DESTROY THE EARTH

BEWARE THE PINK PERIL

The chanting went on and on, endlessly. Matt wondered how they could keep it up. It finally got so loud that he walked away. He rolled up his sleeping bag and sat down on a hunk of marble. He heard the chanting go on:

The Earth is ugly
And it blocks our view.
Let's blow it up
Without further ado.

Well, Matt thought, you can't say things aren't exciting on the Moon. He was just sitting, thinking, when he thought he heard a new sound. It was a kind of humming. What's that, he wondered. Then he felt little bumps on his face and hands. They became bumpier. Pretty soon he saw spots before his eyes. They got bigger. Suddenly he knew. The vogels! The noise of the chanting and the stamping was agitating the tiny, unseen vogels! They were gathering into little lumps, which would gather into bigger ones, which would join into huge ones. They would roll and crush whatever was in their path!

"Stop!" Matt yelled. He waved toward Robinson K. Russo, who paid no attention. "Stop your noise!" Matt started across the crater as fast as he could. But when he reached the mob, they couldn't hear him. "The vogels are coming!" he yelled into Russo's ear.

Russo looked startled, but had no control over his people now. He seemed helpless, just standing there.

"Do something!" Matt warned him. But it was too late. A cloud of dust approached. As it got closer, Matt saw it was a medium-sized band of vogels, rolling, rolling. It ran right into the line of pickets, scattering them, but not crushing anyone. "That was a small one!" Matt yelled at Russo. "Tell your people to shut up or bigger ones will come."

But Russo did nothing, and pretty soon a bigger ball came rolling along. This one ran over a lady Moonster's leg and hurt it. They carried her away, and then the mob realized the danger. But now a dozen big vogel bands that had formed on the heights of the crater came pounding along, bouncing in the air when they hit a rock, and almost floating along toward the Moonsters, whose screaming didn't help any.

"Jump!" Matt cried out. "Get up over them!" But no one listened. Finally, just as the first big ball was about to hit him, he pushed off, and it sailed under him. Then the Moonsters came to their senses. They made use of the low gravity and leaped up high, letting the big vogel balls roll under them, across the flats and up the other side. When the people came down again, some were crying, and others fell down afraid. Then the vogel balls started back again, coming from the other direction.

"Here they come again!" Everybody jumped again, and the vogels went under them, smashing the flag that Kalmuck had put down, but hurting no one. Matt waved his arms at the crowd, trying to signal them to be quiet, but they screamed on and on. Matt looked up the craterside and saw that the dozen balls had formed into one gigantic band of vogels. It was the hugest he had ever seen or even heard of. It stayed there a moment and then slowly inched down the slope, gathering speed. Soon it was lost in the dust it picked up, and all one could see was an enormous cloud coming closer.

"Jump! Jump!" Matt cried. The giant ball went under the crowd, but this time it took a slightly different path across the floor of the crater, and it went straight for the *Apollo*. From up above, Matt saw the heads of Dr. Davinchy and Wiley Kalmuck at the hatch door.

"Get out!" he yelled. They couldn't have heard him, but they saw what was coming, and they scrambled down the ladder lickety-split and ran out of the path of the rolling horror. Then, with a grinding, crunching explosion, the vogel ball flattened the *Apollo* into twisted metal and kept on going.

Matt settled onto the ground again, along with the rest of the crowd. The giant vogel ball was climbing the crater on the other side, slowly but surely. And Matt knew it would come back. "All right, Russo," he told the bewildered fellow. "Get your people out of here quickly." Russo wasted no time, and everyone followed him to the safety of a big cave in the distance.

Matt hurried to the Earthlings, who were dragging along in their lead-filled shoes.

"Oh, my beautiful *Apollo,*" wailed Dr. Davinchy. "All those instruments, wrecked, gone."

"That's not the half of it," growled Kalmuck. "How're we supposed to get back home now?"

"No time for that," Matt said. "That vogel band is coming back and you'd better get off the crater floor." He helped them along so they were out of range when the big thing came speeding across Tycho again. Up the other side, then back down again and up again. Back and forth. Moonsters sat and waited for the vogels to disband. But it would take time for the excited creatures to calm down and separate into the tiny individuals they really were.

Then, above the swish of the vogel ball as it rolled back and forth, another sound was heard. It came from the craggy crater tops.

"Hip-ark! Hip-ark!" It was a bellow, a deep grunting bleat that made the bones of all Moonsters shiver. It was the cry of the giant Hipparchus that roamed freely this part of the Moon. It was hungry. "Hip-ark! Hip-ark!" groaned the unseen monster. Matt listened, and then he saw the vogel band roll up the side of the crater and into the shadows. But this time it didn't roll down again. The cries of the starving Hipparchus ceased. It had found something to eat.

8. A Surprise for Maria

A solemn ceremony was being held in the big cave at Crater Tycho where Chairman R. T. Muss had his temporary office. Spaceman Matthew Looney was the object of the affair. Chairman Muss pinned a fine silver medal upon his uniform and said:

"I hereby award you, in the name of the Moon, the Order of Distinguished Spaceman, for bravery in aiding helpless Moonsters being attacked by a rampaging band of vogels."

Members of Mongress and other officials applauded, and then approached to shake Matt's hand. He smiled, but felt slightly shy about all the attention.

"Thank you, sir," he said in a short speech. "I only did my duty as I saw it." (Matt already held the Sky Medal with Lava Cluster, for his voyage to Earth.)*

But that wasn't all. Chairman Muss then signaled an aide, who opened a stone door to let in a man wearing the uniform of Space Admiral.

"Uncle Lucky!" exclaimed Matt. "When did you get here?" He snapped to attention and saluted.

Admiral Looney smiled. In his hand was a parchment. Without answering Matt's question, he began:

"Repeat after me: 'I, Matthew Looney, do swear to uphold the honor and obey the regulations of the Space Navy . . .' "

Matt repeated the words.

" '. . . and to faithfully discharge the obligations of Space Commander.' "

Matt's knees shook a little as he finished the oath. Admiral Looney saluted *him,* and handed him the parchment. Matt unrolled it and there were the orders, all right. Matt couldn't believe it. Jumped two grades to Commander! You had

---

* See *Matthew Looney's Voyage to the Earth.*

to be master of your own spacecraft to justify such a high rank.

"Gee," he stammered, "I—well, thank you. But—why?"

His uncle put an arm around the young fellow's shoulders, leading him to a bench and a slate conference table, where they sat down. The others did likewise.

"Matt, they called me here not only to promote you to Commander—which I was proud to do—but also to seek my advice on how to deal with the Earth problem. Chairman Muss has told me of the decision of Mongress, which has not been announced yet, and in which you will take a big part."

"What is that?" Matt asked.

"We shall colonize one of the satellites we discovered in Hercules and establish a spatial base there. That will give us a means of outflanking Earth in case of any military action. It will put us in a stronger position."

"How could we be in a stronger position? When the Lava-Four destroys Eta Ursae Majoris, Earth will leave us alone."

"The Lava-Four has already turned that star into gas," the Admiral said.

"Well?" Matt asked. "Isn't that proof enough of our position?"

"We can't prove it to the Earthmen."

"Why not?"

"Because last night, when the vogels ran wild . . ."

"You mean—?"

"That's right, son."

"Crushed the astroputer with all our sight and sound recordings of the event?"

"Yes."

"Oh, no!" Matt slapped his forehead.

Chairman Muss broke in. "And they have made it plain that they not only don't believe in our military power, but that their tribe—the Unplied Snakes of A Merrygo, or whatever they call it—is prepared to use deadly weapons to force their way here, if need be. Apparently there is great rivalry among Earthmen to see who can claim the Moon for themselves. Well, we've got to be prepared for such foolishness. We've got to build more Lava-Fours, for example, and be ready to fire them."

"Well," Matt smiled, "that Enchilada is a wonderful spot for that sort of thing. I'm sure whoever goes there will get along fine."

"And your job, Commander," said the Chairman, "will be to lead the caravan of spaceships to the new colony."

"Me? What about Uncle Lucky—I mean, Admiral Looney?"

"He must stay here as Commander-in-Chief of the Space Navy."

"Whew! That's a big order. How many will be going? What ships will we use? How soon do we—?"

"Wait a moonit, Matt," laughed his uncle. "We'll get into all that at your next briefing. Let's relax awhile."

Relax, thought Matt. *How could I relax at a time like this?*

The new Commander Matthew Looney soon found out more about the plans and his responsibility. The residents of the Moon were told about the decision, and volunteers were called for to make the space trek to Hercules. Moonsters love to travel, and many responded. There were young and old; there were just plain adventurers, and there were entire families looking for a new way of life. There were also the worry-warts who thought that the further from the troublesome Earth, the better. Naturally, there were plenty of Anti-Earthers in that group, including the leader of the Anti-Earth League, Robinson K. Russo, who had his own private spaceship.

Actually, there were only two ships with modern equipment for navigating as far as Hercules. One was the *Ploozer* (named for the famous scientist), which had once made a trip to Earth with Matt and the Admiral. The other was the *Feebey,* which had just come back from the distant cluster. The *Ploozer* would remain on the Moon. The *Feebey,* under the command of Matt, would lead the way, carrying equipment and supplies for establishing a Space Navy base. It would be followed by smaller spaceships, carrying military personnel, technicians, and the civilian Moonsters who had volunteered to emigrate.

The cosmic safari would leave from the Sea of Crisis. The Moon was a busy, busy place preparing for this event. Not only did food and supplies have to be stored for the journey, but enough food had to be carried to keep the colony going in the new land while homes could be built and gardens planted. Many children would be making the trip, and this meant that extra care had to be taken to insure their safety, health, and education.

Crater Tycho, which had been the scene of so much excitement, was practically deserted. The mobs of Moonsters had left for their homes, some of them to prepare for the journey. Robinson K. Russo was busy rounding up a group of his followers to go along with him. Chairman Muss and government officials had returned to Copernicus, the capital. Admiral Looney had removed the two Earthmen to the Sea of Crisis and found a place for them to stay. They had brought with them the broken parts of the *Apollo* radio and tried to put it together so they could call the Earth for help, but so far they had not been successful.

Dr. Davinchy and Wiley Kalmuck were worried about the spot they were in. Their spaceship was wrecked, their means of communication with Earth was gone, and their supply of oxygen would not last forever. It seemed so sudden: one day Kalmuck was planting the flag and claiming the Moon, the next day he and his partner were stranded and helpless. The Earthers saw that there was a lot of activity at the Sea of Crisis spaceport and Space Navy Headquarters, but they didn't understand the language, so they didn't know what it meant.

But the governing officials of the Moon didn't mean to ignore the Earthlings; they assigned Ambassador Hornblower to keep them informed. He went to their quarters to tell them of the plans to colonize Hercules (but not about the military base to be built there; that must be kept secret).

"That's more like it, fella," smirked Wiley Kalmuck. "You people can see the handwriting on the wall, all right. We're going to take over the Moon sooner or later, so's you might as well clear out while the going's good."

"That ain't what I said," Hector Hornblower snapped back at the Earther. "But if you wanna take it that way, what can I do about it?"

Wiley was holding a part of the broken radio in his hand, and he shook it in the young ambassador's face. "Soon's I get this little gadget fixed, I'm callin' out the troops, see? There'll be so many American flags stickin' in the Moon it'll look like a pin cushion. And it'll be ours, all ours!" He broke down into a gleeful cackle that made Hector's spine tingle in spite of himself.

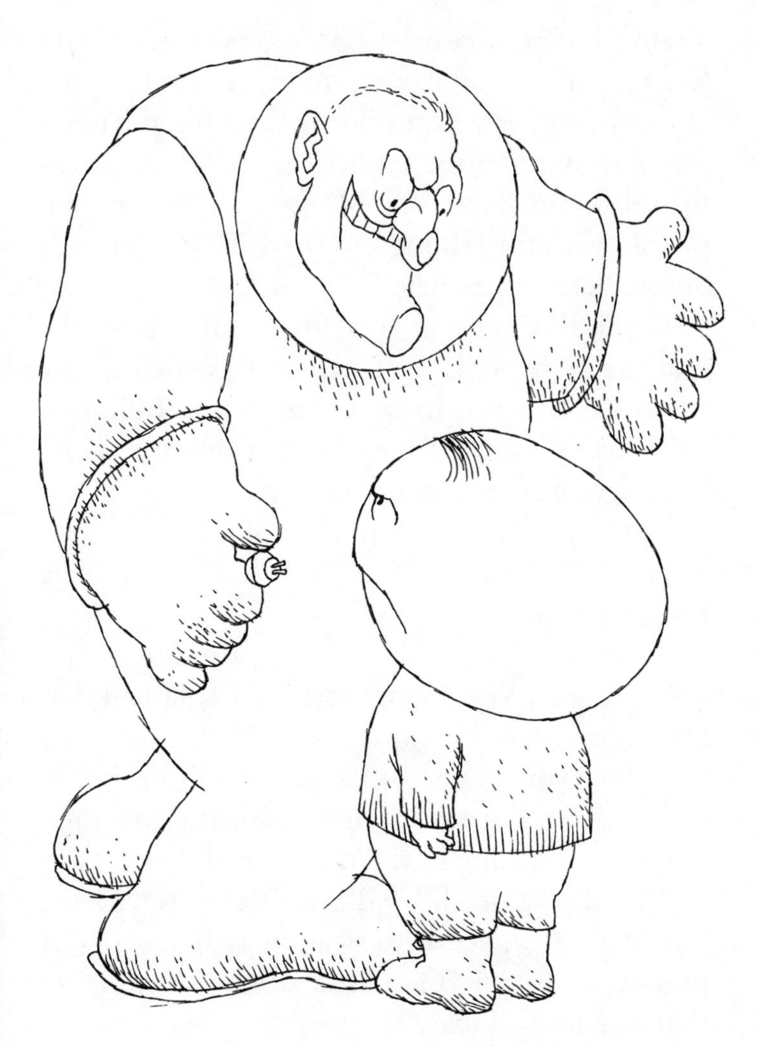

"It'll be ours, all ours!"

Dr. Davinchy touched Hector's arm. "Don't listen to him, Mr. Ambassador. He's rather impetuous. I give you my word that our purposes are mainly scientific, and that our government would never take the Moon away from you people without talking it over with you. That's always been our policy."

Wiley Kalmuck nodded his head vigorously. "That's right, fella. We call it a powwow, like when we talked things over with the Indians."

"Why didn't your government sign the treaty I brought, then?" Hector asked.

"Treaty?" cried Kalmuck. "We love to sign treaties! Don't we, Doc? It just takes a little time, that's all."

"You can't just walk up to the President with a treaty and say, 'Sign here,' " explained Dr. Davinchy.

"Well, you better think of something better than calling out the troops," Hornblower said, "because with our Lava-Four we could—"

"Aw, come on, li'l fella," Wiley interrupted. "You don't expect us to swallow that Lava-Four nonsense, do ya? That stuff about burnin' up that star, and all that?"

"No, I guess I don't, and that's why we ran

that test for you. But it got botched up by them pesky vogels. Lemme tell ya, though, ya better use your radio to get yourselves rescued and that's all—no flags, no troops, or your lopsided planet'll be turned into a lump of nothin'." Hornblower turned and stomped out of the room.

As soon as he was gone, Kalmuck locked the door and turned to his colleague with a big smile. "This is great, Doc! Do you know what this means? We're sittin' pretty. I got me a little plan." He pulled the scientist to him and whispered into his ear.

While the two Earthers were thus engaged, another conspiracy was being hatched elsewhere on the Moon. Deep in a hidden cave, the Anti-Earth League met secretly. Robinson K. Russo spoke to his followers. His big, misshapen head rolled from side to side.

"Moon-lovers and Earth-haters," he said, "we cannot depart from our little planet without evening up the score."

"Yay!" they cheered.

"For a long time we have done our best to talk our fellow Moonsters into getting rid of the Earth. Our talking did no good. Now it is too late for talk, my friends. *It is time for action!*"

"Russo! Russo! Hail, Russo!"

"I call now for volunteers. Six young, healthy chaps who will put into effect my plan for revenge!"

"Take me!"

"Me!"

"Here I am, Russo!"

Dozens had jumped to their feet. After careful testing and questioning, six were chosen. The meeting ended; these six remained. Their leader told them of his scheme, rehearsed them, and later, dressed in black and carrying mysterious equipment and tools, with Robinson K. Russo leading, they sneaked out of the cave and across the lunascape. They disappeared in the gloom.

On another part of the Moon, in the cool cave at 22 Zinc Road, Crater Plato, the Looney family was trying to keep a stiff upper lip at the thought of Matt going away again.

"You'll be gone for good, and we'll never see you again," Mrs. Looney sniffled.

"Aw, that's not true," Matt told her. "The

Feebey will have to make regular ferry trips back and forth. I'll see you then. And when Dad retires from the Powder Works, you all will move to Enchilada. Wait till you see it. It's really nice."

Mr. Looney chuckled. "Why, son, there will always be a Looney at the Powder Works. The younger generation can't seem to understand that. On your next visit, you'll find your sister, Maria, here, taking over. She's going to be the finest little old powder gal you ever did see. Right, honey?"

Maria smiled weakly. "Sure, I guess so. There was a time when I thought of traveling, but I suppose it's silly."

"That's the idea," Matt said. "There's no place in space for girls, anyway. They get starsick and are always wanting to go back home, and we're going to have enough problems with the urchins on board, without taking along the Commander's *sister*."

Maria's green eyes flashed at her brother. "Well, really! I could hold my own out there just as well as you could, smarty!"

"Now, now, children, this is no time for fighting," sniffled their mother. "Maria's going to stay here and keep us company, while Matt's away. Come on, let's sit down and enjoy our meal. It will be our last one together for a long time."

Clong, clong. The sound of the iron knocker on the stone front door!

"Who could that be?" Mrs. Looney hurried to answer. When she returned to the living room she was with an elderly stranger who carried a briefcase. He opened it, took out some papers, and cleared his throat.

"Ahem. I am from the Cosmic Comfort Corps. Is a Miss Maria Looney here?"

Maria's eyes widened.

"Answer the nice man, dear," her mother said. "Yes, sir, this is our Maria."

"I am pleased to announce, Miss Looney, that your application has been accepted and that you have been named Flight Librarian for the Hercules migration. You should be ready to depart immediately for a short training program at the Mooniversity, and from there to the Sea of Crisis for the takeoff. Now if you will just sign here . . ."

Mrs. Looney fainted, hitting the hard floor with a terrible thump before Matt and his father could reach her. They laid her out on the pebble couch and then both spoke at once.

"What *is* this, young lady?"

"Flight Librarian? You?"

Maria's face showed shock and surprise, but as her father and brother stared at her, amazed and hoping she would say it was all a big mistake, her feelings changed. She took the stylus held by the CCC chap and signed, as if to say, *What do you think of that?* The two Looney men remained speechless. The newcomer spoke again, handing the papers to the father.

"And now, sir, if you will co-sign this agreement. We've had a little trouble with underage Moonsters joining the Corps without permission. Of course, you signed your daughter's application, but still—red tape and all that."

"You say I signed the—um—appli—?" He couldn't finish the sentence.

Maria looked her father straight in the eye. "Yes, Daddy, don't you remember?"

"Of course, if you *didn't,*" the CCC fellow said, laughing, fishing out the application itself, "and this were a forgery, then we'd send this pretty young girl to jail. But this *is* your signature, isn't it, sir?"

Mr. Looney sighed. "Certainly, certainly. Here, give me that stylus."

Papers in order, the Corpsman left. From the pebble couch, Mrs. Looney groaned. "Where am I? What happened?" She sat up.

"It's nothing, Diana, only that your daughter is going to Hercules, too."

"Ohhhhh." Mrs. Looney swooned again. This time they caught her.

9. Hijackers

"Now, Maria," said the instructor at the Cosmic Comfort Corps Training School at the Mooniversity, "today we shall take up the operation of the rapid intelligence machine, or the Brainpusher, as it is better known."

He pointed to a box with some handles and lights and wires sticking out here and there. He lifted it onto a table and had Maria sit before it. He took the white wire and attached it to her head behind her right ear, and took the black wire and attached it to her left ear. Then he went to a shelf and took down a red ball about the size of a small meteorite. He opened a tiny door in the machine.

"The red balls are for history, the green ones for mathematics, the blue ones for science, and so on. You'll get to know them soon enough." He pushed the red one into the slot and closed the tiny door. "Now, after you put the ball into here, you switch the power on, you turn this knob, and you fix it so you get not too much and not too little of the subject you are teaching. Here, I'll set this at Two."

Maria felt a humming go through her skull. The instructor turned off the Brainpusher.

"I don't seem to have learned anything," she remarked.

"You can't, when you're wide awake," he explained. "Too much mental interference. That's why we have these sleeping pills. Take one for each ball. You'll doze off and all the lessons will be a part of your memory when you wake up." He showed her a jar of spotted capsules.

"You mean we're taking the Brainpusher to Hercules?"

"That's right. It will be used on the voyage, too, to keep the students busy and so they won't fall behind. There'll be a special School Rocket in the caravan, and you, as Flight Librarian, will be in charge of teaching."

"Why don't we just attach the Brainpusher to the kids' ears, and let them learn everything that way?"

"Oh, you must be joking," laughed the instructor. "If we did that, all the youngsters would know everything that the grown-ups do, and we'd have a terrible time bossing them around. We have enough trouble as it is, controlling the little—um—Moonsters, without making them our intellectual equals. Right?"

"I guess so," Maria agreed halfheartedly.

While Maria was going through the CCC course, many others on the Moon were also making ready for the voyage. Commander Matthew Looney, with the help of Professor Ploozer, worked day and night on the details for the flight. In addition to the big ones, many smaller and private ships had to be put in shape. Wealthy Moonsters made room in their space yachts to carry passengers, and some families with small vehicles added extra engines for the star trek. All of them, of course, would have to follow behind the *Feebey,* or else they would quickly get lost in space.

The day for takeoff eventually came. Moonsters are good organizers, and everything was quite in order. They had sold or rented their caves, they had canceled their magazine subscriptions, and they were saying good-bye to the past and hello to the future.

The many ships were lined up on the large landing field at the Sea of Crisis. Finally, tearful farewells behind them, passengers were on board, the hatches were closed, and there was a rumble as all the engines warmed up. In the *Feebey* were Commander Looney and his crew, along with a large party of scientists and their families. In another craft were Vice-Chairman Heckity and members of Mongress, for instance, and in another were Flight Librarian Maria Looney and her pupils. Robinson K. Russo, in his own spaceship, had Anti-Earth Leaguers with him. They seemed to be quite cheerful.

At Space Expeditionary Headquarters Control and in the observation rooms were many of the Moonsters who had come to see relatives and friends off. Mr. and Mrs. Looney, for instance, and Professor Ploozer and, of course, Admiral Lockhard Looney. At the communications desk, the Professor and the Admiral watched carefully.

"*Feebey* to Control, request permission to

take off," Matt's voice crackled over the speaker.

"Take off when geready," the Professor replied. Out on the field there was a blast of sound and dust as the *Feebey* shot away from the surface. Then, one by one, the others followed. The noise and the clouds of smoke made it difficult for the observers to see. The sky was filled with flying objects. They seemed to grow smaller as they headed for a rendezvous with the *Feebey*. The Sea of Crisis became quiet. In the Headquarters cave, a sniffling could be heard. It was Mrs. Looney. Mr. Looney sat next to her. He looked very sad.

But out there on the bridge of the *Feebey*, there was much activity. Matt was at the helm, while Mr. Bones was at the astroputer. Below them, dust hid the Sea of Crisis. On all sides of them were the circling ships.

"Tell them to fall in behind us as instructed, Mr. Bones," Matt ordered.

Mr. Bones sent the message out over the Interspatial Spectrophone. "I can't keep track of them all, sir," he told Matt. "Let's just hope they follow the plans we gave them."

As far as Matt could tell, the others got in line astern of the *Feebey*, although it was not possible to see behind the big ship very well. He called the engine room for slow ahead, and the caravan began its journey. Later, as they got clear of the Moon, they picked up speed and began cruising at a rate that the others could keep up with.

"Mr. Bones, give me a reading," Matt finally asked.

"Aye, aye, sir." The navigator went to work. "Well, it looks to me as though we must take the Alpha Centauri route," he finally announced. "It's the shortest."

Matt took his eyes off the instruments and looked at Mr. Bones. "What? That takes us right past Earth. That means we'll be pulled off course by gravity."

"Only the big ships, Commander, and we've got our super-AGM's.* The little ones can get by okay."

Matt was silent a moment, then agreed. "Well, all right. We must save fuel."

Soon the engines were stopped, and the *Feebey* and the other ships traveled on momen-

* A large version of the smaller Anti-Gravity Manipulator that each Moonster carried with him to defy gravity on foreign bodies.

tum, as they would until they got closer to Earth. Then they would need power to keep going, but after that it would be clear sailing most of the way to the distant globular cluster called Hercules. The Moon faded in the distance, and the *Feebey* quickly fell into a routine which would be followed throughout the trip. Matt checked with the other ships now and then, and it seemed as if everything was going smoothly.

"Too smoothly," he said to Mr. Bones on the second day out. "I'm superstitious."

"Oh, stop worrying, Commander. Here, I'll take over and you go and get some chow."

So Matt left the bridge and went to the mess hall. He sat at the captain's table, and Wondervon Brown, the cook, brought him the menu.

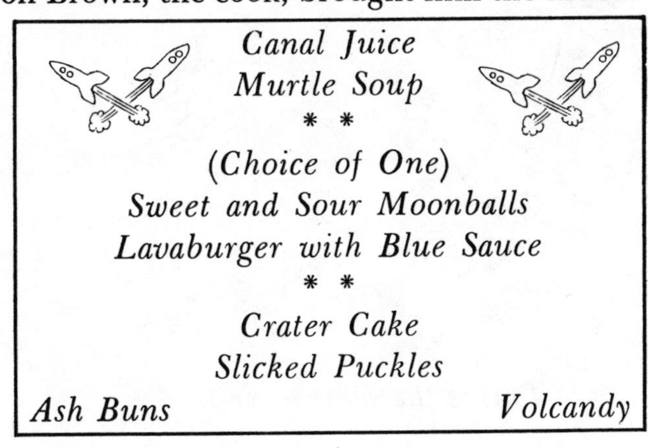

Canal Juice
Murtle Soup
* *
(*Choice of One*)
Sweet and Sour Moonballs
Lavaburger with Blue Sauce
* *
Crater Cake
Slicked Puckles
Ash Buns *Volcandy*

"This is the same as yesterday."

Matt read it in a glance, then looked up at the big, shaggy-haired Brown. "This is the same as yesterday."

The cook's face tightened. He held a big spoon under Matt's nose. "Yah, und it's der same as tomorrow, und der day after dot. Listen, young fellow, I been cooking meals for your uncle on dese trips for years, und he never complained. Ven you vass a little pipsqueak on dat first time ve vent to Earth, you ate vot I put in front of you. Now, do you vant sumting to eat or don't you?"

"Is that any way to talk to your superior?" Matt asked the crotchety old fellow.

"Yah. It's der vay I talk to food complainers, dot's vot."

"All right," Matt sighed, "bring me what I didn't order yesterday." He had to smile as Brown went back to the galley. The man had never forgiven Space Headquarters for making him a cook long ago, after he had caused so much trouble by insisting there was life on Earth. Brown had turned out to be right, but they needed a cook very badly, and no one could be found to take his place, so he couldn't be promoted. And now he had a disposition worse than any mess sergeant in the entire Universe. Matt ate his meal thoughtfully, remembering all the exciting events of his previous voyages into the cosmos. When he was finished, he slowly climbed the ladder toward the bridge, thinking to himself, *well, it looks as though this voyage is going to be a dull one.*

He pushed open the door to the bridge and saw the back of Mr. Bones's head as he stood at the wheel. The very instant at which it occurred to him—*that isn't Bones*—the handle was pulled violently out of his hand, an arm got him into a strong, painful headlock and dragged him forward, and the door slammed behind him. He saw stars and tasted moonballs. His head and throat felt as though they were being crushed. Whoever had hold of him was breathing heavily as he put Matt's arms behind him, tied his hands together, and let him drop onto the iron deck. Only then did Matt come completely back to his senses. Only then did he swallow gulps of welcome vacuum. Only then did he look up to see who was his tormenter. There, grinning down, holding a solar gun in his hand, was the Earthman, Wiley Kalmuck!

"You!" Matt exclaimed.

"Right, Buster. Me." The craggy face broke into a sinister grin.

Matt raised his head off the deck to view the scene. Mr. Bones had been tied up, too, and was seated with his back against a bulkhead and with a disgusted expression. At the wheel was the other Earthman, Dr. Leonard O. Davinchy. Kalmuck lifted Matt to his feet and pushed him, helpless, into one of the cockpit chairs. The young Moonster shouted at him:

"What's it all about? You didn't have to do this. If you wanted to come to Hercules we'd have been glad to bring you. How'd you get on board, anyway? Last I saw of your sourpuss was when we said good-bye at Space Control."

"The old stowaway trick, Buster. And it isn't Hercules we're after, but that little old Earth. That's what it's all about—me and the Doc, here, gettin' back to home, sweet home."

"Is that right?" Matt asked the fat scientist.

"I'm afraid so, Matt," the kindly fellow replied. "I don't like to take part in this violence, but it is absolutely vital that we return to Earth and to our own atmosphere. You see, we're running out of oxygen." He pointed to the tank strapped to his back. "This was our last chance."

"The beauty of it is that no one gets hurt," Kalmuck smiled. "We just set down, jump out, and then let you all go on your way." He waved the barrel of the solar gun at Matt. "As long as you play ball, Buster. Otherwise—" He left the threat unfinished, and Matt had no doubt that Wiley Kalmuck would stop at nothing to further his nefarious scheme.

"You can't do that," Matt objected. "All the other Moon ships will try to land, too, and there'll be accidents and confusion."

"That's tough, Buster. But it's us or them, and I'm in charge. All right, Doc, let's go!"

Dr. Davinchy, unable to speak the language, could not call Engineer Harry Stottle on the phone. He therefore used the manual control. He pressed the *Ready With Engines* button, an answering light flashed from below, and the Earthman slowly turned the wheel and steered the *Feebey* toward the huge, ugly planet.

Matt closed his eyes in despair. He knew that to the stern a long line of trusting Moon vehicles were also turning, following these Pied Pipers to their possible doom.

10. Russo Tells All

Robinson K. Russo's private spacecraft, with the leader of the Anti-Earth League himself in the pilot's seat, wobbled through the heavens. The happy fellow was steering with one hand, and in the other he waved a glass of firmamented canal juice. He was feeling no pain, as they say on the Moon when someone's had too much of the stuff, and he sang songs, badly:

Onward, spacebound Moonsters,
Singing as we go,
With the Anti-Earth flag
Waving to and fro . . .

Crowded around Russo were a lot of Leaguers, and they were having themselves a party, too. In fact, ever since taking off from the Sea of Crisis, everyone on board had been carrying on in this fashion. In the little kitchen they were slicing fancy meats and cracking open new bottles of the giddy firmament. It was, to say the least, utter pandemonium.

"Fill m' glass again, hearties," called Russo, "we got lots t' cebrelate—celeblate—oh, y'know what I mean. Whoops! Watch out f'that asteroid." He spun the wheel and everyone crashed into one side of the room. He spun it back and they all went flying over to the other. "Ugly old Earth, we won't be seein' it no more. Yippee!"

"Yippee!" echoed his happy followers.

On another vehicle in the caravan, things were quiet and peaceful. Maria Looney had just finished conducting a class in Galactic History and sent her students back to their parents' staterooms. She sat down and rested. She smiled to herself.

Imagine that! she thought. *Yesterday I didn't know a thing about Galactic History and today I taught it to a class. Too bad they didn't have something like the Brainpusher when I was starting school. Well, I've got to do science after lunch. Let's see, I'll need this red ball, and put it in here, and turn the dial to Six. Attach the wires. And take this pill. I'll just lie here. Ah, that feels comfy. Hmmm. I wonder. Why don't I turn the dial to Twelve, and I can learn tomorrow's lesson, too. There.*

Maria fell asleep. If she had read the instructions on the back of the Brainpusher she would have been more careful. In one place is written:

> *Attention: Never increase the Input Dial by more than one point at each use. Otherwise massive memory will result.*

Directly behind the *Feebey* came a vessel called the *Moonbeam,* which carried Moon's Vice-Chairman Heckity and a party of minor officials who would set up the colonial government in the Hercules Cluster. They were at this very moment seated in the conference room, settling as many details as they could ahead of time. They were interrupted by a member of the crew.

"Gentlemen, the pilot said to tell you that it looks as though the *Feebey* is going to land on Earth."

"What? That can't be!" cried Heckity.

"He wants to know, should we follow?"

"I can't answer that, young man. Have the pilot contact Commander Looney and get an explanation for this unusual action."

"But, sir, we tried, and there is no answer."

The officials got to their feet in alarm. Heckity declared, "Well, I'll just see about that," and he started for the door. But he was halted by a horn blast over the intercom.

"Attention! All passengers! Fasten safety belts! Prepare for landing!"

They all quickly sat down again. A similar scene could have been observed on each of the other vehicles as the surprising word came of an approaching landing.

On the bridge of the *Feebey* there was tension, as the two Earthlings, unfamiliar with the workings of the Moon craft, attempted to bring her down. Dr. Davinchy was able to use the engines, for Mr. Stottle still was unaware of what was taking place. If any crew members or passengers throughout the ship were suspicious, there was no sign of it. The door to the bridge was locked; no one could get in if they wanted to. Besides, things were happening too fast for them to have done anything, even if they did realize the situation.

"Wiley," called Dr. Davinchy, "get on that astroputer and figure out where we will be landing."

Kalmuck fiddled with the contraption, but couldn't get anywhere with it. He turned to Mr. Bones and pointed the solar gun at him. "How d'ya turn it on?" he snarled.

"That's for me to know and you to find out," the brave Mr. Bones answered.

"Why, you—" Kalmuck pressed the trigger and let a solar pellet fly. It hit right next to the tied-up Moonster and melted a hole in the bulkhead. "The next one'll be a darn sight better shot than that, wise guy."

Matt saw that there was no point in resisting, for it might endanger the entire expedition. "Tell him, Mr. Bones," he said.

So Kalmuck got the astroputer working, fed his data into it, and out came the tape. He took it to Dr. Davinchy, who read it. "The Outback!" he exploded. "I wanted Cape Kennedy, you idiot! Well, it's too late now. Here we go! Hang on!"

It was the worst landing Matt had ever seen. First, Dr. Davinchy called for too much reverse, and then for not enough. The vehicle bounced around like an asteroid out of orbit. Finally, there was one last bounce and that was it: they had landed. Wiley Kalmuck and Dr. Davinchy shook hands, grinned, and rushed toward the cockpit escape hatch. They let themselves into the compression chamber and sealed the inner door behind them.

"Hey, what about us?" yelled Matt. But the two men had already gone out the outside exit. Matt got on his knees and worked his way over to his first mate and untied him. Mr. Bones then freed Matt. They slowly opened the valves in the escape chamber and let in Earth atmosphere.

"Remember our first trip?" Matt grinned. "When we thought this stuff was poisonous?"

In a jiffy they were out onto the surface of the planet Earth. Dr. Davinchy and Wiley Kalmuck were stretching and laughing, then kneeling down, kissing and patting the ground. But Matt paid little attention to them. Instead he watched nervously as the other ships in the caravan came in for landings. Fortunately, the Earth at this point is as broad and smooth as the Sea of Crisis, so there was plenty of room. One by one, they came down. First the *Moonbeam,* which settled

They slowly opened the valves in the escape chamber.

next to the *Feebey* easily, as she was being piloted by an expert pilot. Then the others, of all sizes and shapes, bumped their way to the ground. Two of them tipped over at the last moment, but no one was hurt.

As this was going on, Vice-Chairman Heckity and the others from the *Moonbeam* were gathered in a group along with Matt and the passengers from his flight. Explanations had been made, and the Moonsters grumbled and looked angrily at the two Earthmen, who were off to one side talking intently to each other, and busy fooling with some equipment they had brought, apparently salvaged from the wrecked *Apollo*. As the travelers stepped from their spaceships, they had to turn up their portable AGM's, so that the powerful gravity on the Earth wouldn't prevent them from moving about.

Matt called a meeting of pilots and engineers and talked about the problem of taking off for Hercules again. He asked them to check their ships, and to report about fuel, damage, injuries, et cetera. "Mr. Bones," he asked, "do you recognize this area? It doesn't look like any Earth spot we've been to before."

Bones shook his head in ignorance. Then Matt saw the two Earthmen approaching. "We got the radio working, and reached our Headquarters," Dr. Davinchy said. "They'll send someone to pick us up as soon as they can. Matt, I am sorry to have upset your plans this way, but—"

Matt waved a hand impatiently. "Aw, what good's an apology now? You got us here and we're stuck with it. We'll leave right away. Of course, you could give me an idea where we are, if you know."

"Sure. This is the Outback, a section of the land we call Australia. There's not much to eat or drink here, but there's plenty of room for you to take off again."

"The Outback, eh?" Before Matt could ask another question there was a blast of rockets overhead. Everyone looked up and saw the last space ship coming in sideways. It was the Russo vessel, and it was swerving this way and that. Matt was worried. "My gosh, look at that."

But in spite of the way it was being driven, Russo's ship finally landed. HERCULES OR BUST! was painted on the side. In a few moments the main hatch was flung open and out piled the Anti-Earthers, with their leader in front. They shouted happily and waved their drinking glasses and surrounded Matt.

"Good work, Matthew, my boy. Tha' was a fas' trip, all right," cried Russo. "So this here's Enchilada. Wow, some spot, I'll say. All right, fellas, how about three cheers for our li'l ol' Commander Looney. Hip, hip, hurray—"

But Matt yelled them down. "Quiet! All of you! This isn't Enchilada by a long shot."

Russo looked at him. "Then it's Tamale."

"No, it isn't Tamale, either. We're nowhere near Hercules. We're on the Earth." Matt couldn't help adding, "Your favorite planet." There was laughter from those in the crowd who could overhear. But there was no laughter from Robinson K. Russo, nor from his friends. They had suddenly grown still, and they didn't act silly any more.

"You're kidding," Russo told Matt, "I hope."

Matt shook his head. "Afraid not."

There was silence for a while. The knowledge was sinking in. Then, all at once, Russo and his Anti-Earthers turned and ran full speed, howling and screaming, toward the spaceship they had arrived in.

"Let's get out of here, *quick!*" yelled Russo.

They all began fighting with each other to get into the hatch. They scratched and kicked, and knocked each other down in their frantic attempts to squeeze into the door all at once.

"Hey, wait, wait," Matt called, running after Russo, and grabbing his arm. "Don't take it so hard. We'll all be leaving together pretty soon. You can't navigate in that old kite. You'll get lost out there."

"Let go of me! Take my advice and leave before this whole planet falls to pieces!" Russo shook himself loose and started up the gangway after his friends. But Matt ran after him again and hauled him down. Then he signaled Mr. Bones and others of his own crew for help and they rounded up the other Leaguers.

"Look here, I've had enough surprises for today," Matt told Russo. "Now just tell me what you're talking about."

Russo appeared to have sobered up in a hurry. He fell on his knees. "I beg of you, Commander Looney. Lead us away. Take off now. Hurry. Save our people."

"Not until you explain yourself."

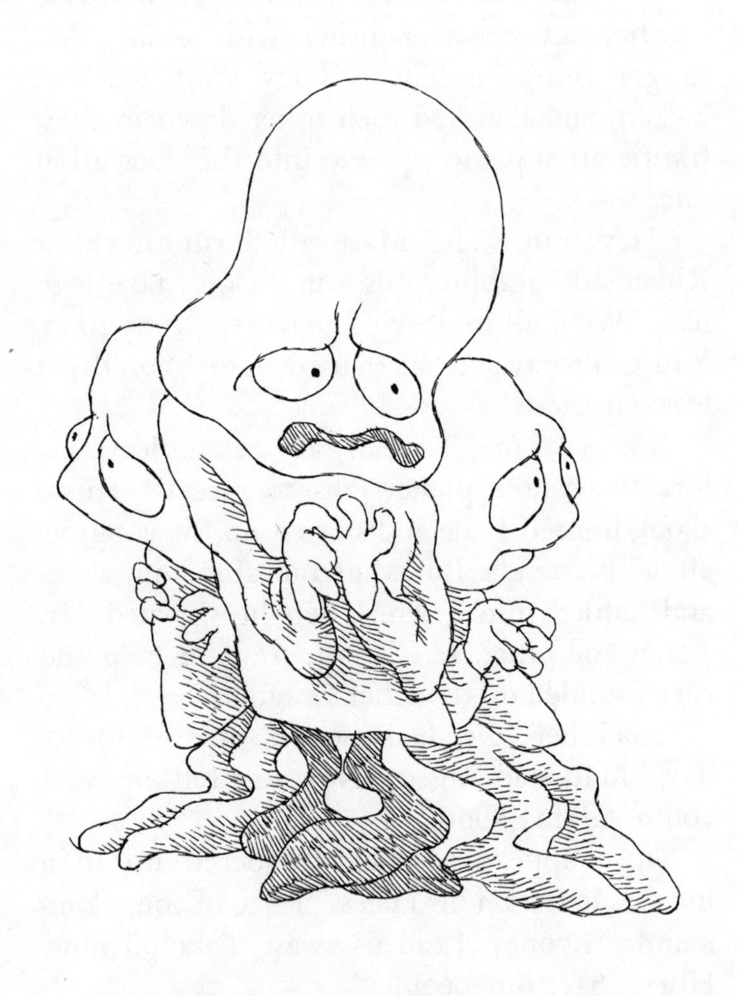

"Oh, oh, oh! It's too awful."

Russo collapsed on the ground. "Oh, oh, oh. It's too awful."

"What's too awful?"

"The Lava-Four," sobbed Russo. "It's on its way."

"On its way to Eta Ursae Majoris? It reached there long ago, as we all know. What's so terrible about that?"

"No, no, the *other* Lava-Four," burbled the unhappy fellow. "The one parked on its launch pad at the Sea of Crisis. It's on its way *here,* to the *Earth!* It will destroy it."

"Come on, Russo, you've had too much firmamented canal juice," Matt said.

"No, ask the fellows. We set a time fuse, so the death-dealing device would blast off at the same time as all our ships did. In the smoke and confusion no one noticed. It's out there now. It's slow, but it'll get here, any day now. And that's the end, poof, of this planet. And us with it. Oh, oh, oh!"

Matt collared a couple of Leaguers. "Is he right?" They were blubbering and shouting, but Matt gathered that Russo was probably telling the truth. They related to him the details of the secret meeting and the six volunteers, led by Russo, who sneaked off in the darkness to arm the Lava-Four for its deadly mission. Matt looked at Russo in disgust. "And so, your hatred of Earth has brought you to this mad scheme. Not only the killing of innocent Earthers, but endangering the lives of your fellow Moonsters, too. You fiend!"

Word of the startling development reached the others. They milled about, scanning the sky for a sign of the dread missile, or hurrying their children into the space ships. Some frightened ones began to ask, "What are we going to do, Commander?" Others crowded around Vice-Chairman Heckity and demanded action. The situation was getting out of hand, Matt feared. He pushed his way through the throng to the side of Vice-Chairman Heckity.

"Calm these people as best you can," he shouted into the official's ear, "while I get through to the Moon for instructions!"

Heckity nodded, and Matt made his way toward the *Feebey*. On the bridge, he turned on the Interspatial Spectrophone, waiting nervously for it to warm up. He glanced out of the spaceshield and saw the Moonsters surrounding Heckity. Finally the main tube of the Spectrophone glowed red, and Matt grabbed the microphone.

"*Feebey* calling Moon Monitor. Come in, please."

He repeated the signal a few times, and finally he got an answer from the communications center in Mooniversity Heights, the very one that the Looney family had visited when Matt was returning from Hercules. He asked to be put in immediate contact with Admiral Looney, and a moment later his uncle's face appeared on the screen.

"Ah, there you are, Matt. We were wondering when you would report in. We've kind of lost your picture in the general excitement here. How is the Hercules migration coming along?"

"You mean you haven't followed our course?" Matt asked. "You don't know our present location?"

The Admiral looked apologetic. "It's our job to track you, I know, but something else interfered. You're going to find this hard to believe, Matt, but our only remaining Lava-Four bomb has been shot off into space. We spent a lot of time locating it, and finally discovered it wobbling around out there, but we have no idea what its target could be. We're just hoping she doesn't turn around and drop down on us! And on top of that, the two Earthmen are missing. I'm telling you, Matt, it's a mystery that has us baffled. You don't look very surprised."

"I'm not," Matt replied. "It's no mystery to me." And he quickly explained to his uncle what had happened to the space travelers. It was Admiral Looney who was surprised.

"I knew we should have locked up those Earthmen! Between them and that troublemaker Russo we're really in a fix, aren't we? Both the Lava-Fours gone. Puts us in rather a bad spot when it comes to a showdown with Earth. These Lava-Threes are no good for blasting such a big planet. Hmmm."

Matt fidgeted while his uncle mused and then said, "Uncle Lucky, we've got a crowd of frightened Moonsters here, wondering when the bomb will drop. You've got to figure some way to stop it and save not only us but all the innocent people on Earth, too."

"Ah, yes, right you are, Matt. Now it usually takes a while for a lava bomb to fuse up. I'll confer with our armament people here and call you right back."

Matt left the Spectrophone and stuck his head out of the hatch. The Moonsters finally spied him and turned from Vice-Chairman Heckity.

"What shall we do?" shouted one Moonster.

"Let's clear out of here, Commander!" called another.

I've got to keep them from panic, Matt thought to himself. He raised a hand, and a hush came over the scared Moonsters.

"Everything's going to be all right," he called out. "Admiral Looney and the specialists just told me there's nothing to worry about." It was a fib, but Matt felt it was necessary. And it seemed to work. There was a murmur among the mob as they talked among themselves, and a few drifted away. Matt had just let out a sigh of relief when there was a hollering from the edge of the crowd.

"Here she comes!"

A Moonster was pointing overhead. Everyone looked up to see a tremendous fat object plodding through the sky. It was the Lava-Four, its sinister black shape spouting orange flames. There was a roar, and the ground seemed to shake. Matt couldn't help it, but his heart pounded in fear. *Was this the end?* Little Moonsters ran to their mothers. Grown-ups screamed, or stood their ground bravely. Others ran pell-mell across the flat desert, or scrambled into their spaceships. But the Lava-Four slowly passed overhead, and then seemed to climb higher above the planet as it disappeared into the distance.

Matt staggered into the cabin and fell into a seat, exhausted. *It'll come back,* he thought. *It'll come back. How much time have we? How much time, before we are all burned to a crisp?*

11. *A Dangerous Situation*

With a Lava-Four floating around you, you don't stall around feeling sorry for yourself, and Matt soon pulled himself together. The end of the day had come; when he poked his head out of the hatch and scanned the sky for further signs of the bomb, it was almost dark. He saw nothing of the ominous rocket-engine flames above, but he did hear faintly nearby the whimpering of children and the angry voices of adults. A rattle of footsteps on the ladder of the *Feebey* announced the arrival of a group of Moonsters, led by Vice-Chairman Heckity.

"Commander Looney," the official declared, "the people are growing hysterical. That terrible weapon may strike at any time. I insist that we continue our journey to Hercules at once." The others murmured in agreement. Matt ushered them all into the cabin, and he tuned in the Spectrophone while he replied:

"Gentlemen, I am as anxious as you are to do that. It is sad to reflect upon the awful fate that awaits those who live on Earth, but we must think of our own kind first." The young Commander fiddled with the dials. "I am just about to call Moon Monitor and report. I suggest you alert your flight crews for takeoff." The visitors prepared to leave, when the crackle of the Spectrophone brought them to a halt. Admiral Looney's face appeared on the screen.

"Calling the Hercules expedition. Come in, please."

Matt quickly responded. "It's me—Matt. Commander Looney, I mean. Sir, the Lava-Four threatens, and I'm giving the order for blast-off."

The Admiral's sharp reply rang through the *Feebey*'s bridge. "Countermand that order Commander! Your party will remain on Earth for further instructions."

"What?" cried Vice-Chairman Heckity. "Tell him we're going anyway. Our lives are at stake."

A knot of Moonsters gathered around the Spectrophone, unbelieving.

Before Matt could say another word, the Admiral spoke again. "I heard that remark. The lives of bullions of Earthers are at stake, too, and it's the fault of a Moonster. Our duty is to exert our utmost to save them. We may need your help, and you must stay there in case we do."

"But—but, the bomb! You mean we—" Matt sputtered.

He was interrupted by his uncle. "The Lava-Four, according to our experts, will circle the Earth three times while its trigger warms up, at the approximate rate of one orbit per day. Then, at some time during the fourth orbit and on the fourth day, it will plunge downward and explode its helio-activated lava all over the globe. Now we cannot just abandon the planet, ugly as it is, to that fate. Our technicians are this very moonit working on a means of disarming or diverting the Lava-Four. As soon as we discover it, you will be told what to do. In the meantime, you have tomorrow and the next day to polish brass and get things shipshape."

"My gosh, Uncle Lucky!" cried Matt. "We're

shipshape now, but we won't be if that hot rock falls on us. What if it warms up on the third day, instead of the fourth? Isn't there some safer place for us to wait? Couldn't we all come back home?"

"Commander Looney, those are your orders," the Admiral said sternly, "and you'll follow them. Remember, officers in the Space Navy can be *de*moted as well as *pro*moted. That is all. Over and out."

Matt bit his lip. "Yes, sir." He switched off the Spectrophone. "Well, there's your answer, gentlemen. Go explain that to the people. I'm going to try to get some rest." The Moonsters grumbled and left the *Feebey*. Matt went to his quarters and flopped onto his bunk. He was so tired he fell asleep right away. He didn't even hear the voice of Vice-Chairman Heckity blaring over the intercom speaker, passing on to all Moon travelers the orders just received.

When Matt awoke the next morning, he peered out the porthole. The sun was shining brightly. He dressed and hurried below to the galley, where the rest of the crew, already eating breakfast, greeted him. Harry Stottle, Chief Engineer, apologized again for having been fooled the day before by Dr. Davinchy and Wiley Kalmuck.

"It's not your fault, Mr. Stottle," Matt assured him. "You couldn't have known the ship was being hijacked while you were down there in the engine room. By the way, I wonder where those two Earthmen are now. They sure disappeared in a hurry after we landed."

"Who cares about them, Commander?" Mr. Stottle growled. "We've got our own skins to worry about."

Matt managed to smile, but it wasn't easy. He finished up his dish of starflakes, excused himself, and went outside. The Moonships rested on the flat surface of the Outback. Technicians and mechanics bustled about making adjustments, in case the order to blast off were given. Passengers huddled in groups near their ships, as though afraid to stray very far. They nervously glanced at the sky, and they kept their children from wandering. Matt approached one of these groups; he noted their anxious faces.

"Why isn't this child in school?" he asked a mother.

She pulled her little girl toward her. "Because it's too dangerous. If you think I'm going to let

Nellie out of my sight today, Mister Commander Looney, you've got another think coming, you and your Lava bombs."

Another mother spoke up. "Isn't that just like you military people! Expose women and children to peril for no reason at all." She grabbed her little boy by the arm. "Marvin, tell the man why you're not in school."

"Because, why should I go to school the day before we all get ourselves killed?"

The boy's loaded question got the other Moonsters stirred up even more. They began their grumbling and threatening again. "Now, look here," Matt declared angrily, "this is absolute nonsense. Our voyage to Hercules has only been delayed a day or two, that's all. Let's get these kids into their classes, where they belong. Where's our Flight Librarian?"

"In the School Rocket," Marvin's mother informed him.

"Well, you women take your children there and tell Miss Looney to keep them busy. We're going to have enough problems without a bunch of wild brats running around loose."

Glaring at him, the mothers reluctantly obeyed. Matt then gave orders that all Moonsters of the right age should be sent to school and attendance taken. Anyone absent would need to show a written excuse to Commander Looney or Vice-Chairman Heckity. With that headache out of the way for the time being, Matt knew that there would be another coming along, and another and another, until the Lava bomb was defused or until the anxious Moonsters were spaceborne again.

"After all," one of them reminded him, "we signed up for a trip to Hercules, not to Earth."

"How can they be so sure it takes three days for the bomb to warm up?" another Moonster asked.

Matt, who had to look optimistic no matter what his real thoughts were, replied cheerfully, "They're experts."

"Experts can be wronger than anyone," somebody said sarcastically. "That monster could come swooping down any moonit and plaster us all."

Before the young Commander could think of an answer to that one, something unfortunate took place. A Moonster who was watching the sky saw a speck in the distance. It came closer and began to give off a throbbing sound. "The bomb!" he cried thoughtlessly, and the panic was on again. Matt knew it wasn't true, but there was nothing he could do to stop them all from screaming and running uselessly for some protection. Matt recognized from past experience that the approaching object was a jet ship used by Earthers to travel from one part of their planet to another. He climbed into the *Feebey,* got out his spyglass, and watched the scene. The winged ship flew along the desert, bounced to a landing, and finally rolled to a stop about half a lunacule away. The numerous passengers who got out were Earthers. Then, to Matt's surprise, two figures emerged from the distant landscape and greeted the newcomers. They were Wiley Kalmuck and Dr. Leonard O. Davinchy, who had obviously hidden overnight in the desert, perhaps fearful of bodily harm at the hands of disgruntled Moonsters.

So that's where they were, Matt reflected, *and someone's come to rescue them. I guess they got their radio working. Now, maybe they'll all go away and leave us to our own worries. I've seen enough of Earthmen for the time being. Oh, no, they're coming this way, all of them. How can I explain about the Lava-Four to them?*

Vice-Chairman Heckity and Commander Looney received the party of Earthmen in the main saloon of the *Feebey*. There were seats for some; others had to stand. There were many introductions, but Matt couldn't remember which name went with which face. It was just a mob of Earthers with crazy skin colors. None of them had the healthy pallor of Moonsters.

"State your business quickly, gentlemen," Matt said at the outset. "We're anxious to get on with our own affairs."

"Ahem," Dr. Davinchy started out, "perhaps I can speak for the others. Your arrival has caused great excitement on Earth, Matt, and these men would like very much to inspect your spaceships for scientific purposes."

"I think that can be arranged," Matt stated. "Of course, we cannot allow anyone on board our vehicles, but a brief external inspection will be acceptable."

Wiley Kalmuck leaped to his feet. "Now, wait a second, fella, who do you think you are? I promised them a look at the whole kit and kaboodle, and if our boys want to get inside your spaceships, you're darn well gonna let 'em, or else!"

Kalmuck's outburst broke the ice, and other

excited Earthers came forward, pushing their way into a tight circle around the Moonsters, or milling about in confusion.

"Hey, Commander Nooley, fifty thousand dollars for a by-line story on your adventures in the Universe!" a man yelled.

"Make it seventy-five, plus screen rights!" another one cried, elbowing his way into the gang. Matt backed up, as the pushing and shoving got more intense. Another group had surrounded Heckity. A fellow with very long hair was waving a sheet of paper and a writing instrument under the Vice-Chairman's nose and made himself heard over the noise. "I'm Hutton, the travel guy! We want exclusive rights to the Moon territory and we're willing to pay plenty for it! Don't listen to anyone else! We can deliver year-round tours! You'll clean up! Sign here!"

Matt's feet were almost off the ground in the press. At one point he felt his ear being pulled. "Ouch!" he cried. A big chap had his mouth right up to it and his voice boomed inside Matt's aching head. "Hey, wha' kinda lube ya use in those flyin' machines of yours? I'm from Greezoil Company. We'll make it worth your while if ya'll switch to usin' Greezoil. It's safe, fast, efficient. Whaddya say? Ten thousand advance. Cash in hand."

"I don't think so," Matt told him.

"Twenty thousand!" the oilman was screaming when he was knocked aside. He finally let go of Matt's ear. When the young Moonster tried to rub it, he found that because of the throng he couldn't free his arm from his side. The next thing he knew, his shirt was being torn open and an Earthman with black tubes sticking out of his ears was putting a round metal disc on his chest. Matt saw that the tubes were connected with the disc. *He's going to kill me,* was Matt's first thought. *He's shooting some poison out of his ears and into my system!* Before he could do anything about that, the fellow pushed up Matt's sleeve and started wrapping a strap around his arm. He squeezed a bulb and Matt thought his arm was going to blow up. He tried to jerk away, but he was hemmed in.

"Hey, what are you doing? Stop!"

The Earther turned and pressed his face close to Matt's. His grin revealed sharp, pointed teeth.

"I am a doctor. We want to know exactly what

makes you tick," he explained. He squeezed the bulb some more and Matt's arm hurt. Finally the grinning doctor with his equipment was gone and his place taken by a bearded man who reminded Matt of Professor Ploozer.

"My dear boy," this one said, "I am a rocket scientist. I am very interested to know how you gain such great thrust from such small engines. I do hope you will change your mind and let us examine the power unit of your fine ship."

Other bearded men had gathered, too, and they echoed that thought. But the jostling and noise was so bad that Matt just couldn't think about an answer. Besides, there were flashes of light that blinded him each time they went off. Someone was making pictures of the scene, apparently. Matt began to feel faint. He saw a crewman pressed against the wall, near a door. He signaled for help, and saw the fellow leave. There was more pushing and shoving. Wiley Kalmuck himself had just taken hold of Matt's arm and was snarling at him when the huge figure of Wondervon Brown loomed in the door. In one hand was a big soup spoon and in the other an iron bar for opening murtle shells. The chef's voice was as big as his form, and he let out

"We want to know what makes you tick."

a bellow that might have been heard back in Crater Plato. The Earthmen fell silent as the big fellow hovered over them. He held up his kitchen weapons and growled like a bear.

"Heraus mit you! Outen! Schnappen ze feeten!"

He took a step forward. The Earthers huddled into a clutch and took a step backward. Brown moved closer. They moved back again. Inch by inch, the chef forced the subdued intruders to the head of the ladder, and one by one, they quickly went down it and away, leaving only a few Moonsters on the deck of the Moonship.

"We'll be back, and don't you forget it!" Wiley Kalmuck warned as he left.

Brown smiled, pleased with the job he had done, and went back to the galley. Matt and Vice-Chairman Heckity fell into a couple of chairs, exhausted. Matt began to cough and choke.

"Oh, this filthy oxygen is too much for me!" he said. He reached for his helmet with vacuum tank, slipped it over his head, and breathed deeply. "Ah!" After a few more moments he put the apparatus aside.

"I can only go so long inhaling this rotten air," he explained to Heckity.

"It doesn't bother me," Heckity said.

"I must be allergic to it."

The two of them were quiet, enjoying the silence, when Heckity mused, "Rather nice to have Wondervon Brown come along. He's not such a good cook, but he makes a fine bouncer."

I wish he could bounce that Lava-Four out of the Universe, so we could go on our way."

Heckity got up. "Commander, we can't sit here like this. We've got work ahead of us. Get our people organized, packed, and all that. Look, get in touch with home and see what they've found out."

Matt went wearily to the Spectrophone again and tuned in. In a few moments he was calling Moon Monitor, making contact. Admiral Looney soon appeared.

"Matt, my boy," he said cheerfully. "I'm glad you called. I think we're on the right track. Ploozer and his staff now believe that the Lava-Four is picking up speed, and that it will go shooting off into the cosmos and cause no harm. Have you seen it make its second orbit yet?"

"No, I haven't," answered Matt.

"Ah, that's a very good sign. Now, listen to me carefully, Matt. Watch for it. And if you don't see the Lava-Four again, rest assured she's out of the way for good."

Matt smiled broadly. "Gee, Uncle Lucky, that's wonderful." After exchanging a few more messages, the two stations signed off. Heckity and Matt happily relayed the news to the other Moonsters. The rest of the morning and part of the afternoon was a pleasant time, and every moment that went by without sight of the Lava bomb made it even more pleasant.

But it was too good to be true. Late in the day Matt was soaking in a nice cool moondust bath when there was a hammering at the stateroom door.

"Commander Looney! Are you there?" It was the voice of Vice-Chairman Heckity.

"Yes, what is it?"

The door was flung open and Heckity stuck his head in, alarm written on his face. "The Lava-Four! It just made its second pass! And it's *closer,* and going *slower,* than before!"

12. A Planet Is Doomed

Well, back to the old drawing board, eh? It was the morning of his third day in the Outback, and Matt lay in his bunk for a while after waking. His uncle's words kept haunting him. "Back to the old drawing board." That's what the Admiral had replied when Matt had told him that the bomb was still very much with them. *He is taking it so lightly,* Matt thought. *I'll just bet if he were here, he wouldn't think it was so funny.*

Matt yawned as he got out of bed. He had spent a sleepless night, not only from reflecting on his uncle's flip attitude, but also because his phone rang constantly with Moonsters calling from the other ships, asking a million questions about this and that. Furthermore, there had been the constant racket of those jet ships coming and going. Matt looked out of the porthole toward the area where the Earthers had set up camp, and sure enough, there were a dozen more of their so-called airplanes, and tents and campfires all over the place. It reminded him of Crater Tycho when the *Apollo* arrived, Matt decided. *I sure hope I can avoid all those screwballs today,* he thought. *I'll just keep out of sight. I've got to stick by the Spectrophone. I want to be here when the final word comes on what to do about this pesky Lava bomb. One more orbit today and then—whew!—we'll be playing with hot lava.* Matt shivered at the prospect.

Matt couldn't have avoided the Earthers that third day any more than he could have swallowed the Purple Pits of Polaris. They came straggling across the flatland and swarmed around the Moonships. Some were officials and some were apparently just people. The first wave appeared in a tight little group led by Hutton, the tour guy. He had a loudspeaker in one hand and he walked backward through the landing area, talking and pointing, followed by all these Earthmen and Earthwomen. At first they were shy and stuck together, but soon they became bolder, peeking into the windows where Moonsters were getting dressed, or climbing into Moonships and introducing themselves. Matt learned about their presence when a large female burst into the *Feebey* and asked for his autograph.

"We're the Tokyo tour," she gushed, "diverted to the Outback." Matt gently pushed her out and locked the hatch, after stamping his name in her diary. But there was no way to keep out of their way when he went outside, as he often had to in the course of his duties. Not only the tourists, but the same excited scientists and reporters from the day before were all over the place. And there were also Moonsters following him around, demanding to know when the space caravan to Hercules would take off, and when they could get out from under the threat of the terrible Lava-Four.

There was one very weird part of the whole picture: *not a single Earthling realized that a circling weapon was prepared to destroy the planet*. For one thing, in the excitement of the

"I think it's only fair to inform them of the danger."

visit by the Moonships, little attention had been given to the bomb's two appearances. Those who wondered had decided that it was just another space vehicle. Then, of course, neither Matt nor any of his fellow travelers had really had a chance to explain the whole business to the Earthlings, although they talked about doing it.

"I think it's only fair to inform them of the danger," Vice-Chairman Heckity declared.

"I beg to differ," Matt said. "I know these Earthers better than you do. In the first place, they just wouldn't believe in the Lava-Four. We can't prove that we vaporized Eta Ursae Majoris, you see. Secondly, Earth people are wild and unpredictable. No telling what they might try to do to us if we told them the story of Robinson K. Russo and how he fired our second bomb at them."

"Well," the Vice-Chairman responded, "if you really think —"

"What they don't know won't hurt 'em," Matt continued. "Look, we'll be hearing from home any moonit, and the whole affair will have blown over. So why upset things any more than they are?"

It added up to a strange scene in the Outback.

Milling about were the Moonsters, worried and nervous about their future, and the Earthers, who were having a wonderful time. As the day wore on, and as more of the airplanes arrived, the area got really jammed, and it was necessary for Matt to call for a volunteer posse to keep order. Most of the fellows who joined the group were Anti-Earthers, and they were really tough in keeping control of the mob. This made some of the visitors angry and there were apt to be little pushing and shoving matches.

"Why don't you go back where you came from?" an Earther shouted at a Moonster once.

The Moonster didn't get a chance to answer that question, as much as he would have liked to. The fact is, a good many of the Earth's inhabitants were wondering why the Moonsters had landed. Only a very few of them were able to get to the Outback, either as tourists, scientists, or whatever. At first they were curious. As time went on, they and the rest of the world began asking questions similar to the one shouted by the angry Earther. Why are the Moonsters here? What do they want? Why don't they leave? Et cetera. The policy of Commander Looney and of Vice-Chairman Heckity was to say as little as possible. Unfortunately, the policy had to be changed, and by the end of that third day, it was a brand new ball game.

The first sign Matt had that things were not going as he had planned was when Leonard O. Davinchy and Wiley Kalmuck showed up. Matt ushered them in to the *Feebey*'s main cabin and offered them seats. Dr. Davinchy accepted, while Wiley Kalmuck snarled, "I prefer to stand, thank you. If you think I'm gonna sit on one of your lousy—"

"Wiley! Please! Let me handle this!" the other Earthman ordered.

The skinny one was silent while the short, fat scientist spoke.

"Matt, the world is in an uproar. Two days ago your fleet of spaceships entered our atmosphere and landed here."

"It's not my fault."

"We won't argue about that. The fact is, you are here, and the entire world knows about it. Except for your two previous expeditions, which came and went almost before they could be noticed, this is the first time that any residents of another place in the Universe have actually stopped on our territory."

"Oh, I can't believe that," Matt said. "Why, there have been travelers in the cosmos for as far back as we can count."

"Well, not in our neck of the woods," the scientist told him.

"How far back do your records go?"

"About a thousand years or so, I guess."

"How long is your year?" the Moonster asked. "I forget."

"The time it takes the Earth to go around the sun once."

"Is that all? A thousand of those? Well, your records are quite incomplete, I can tell you. We know positively that once there was a colony of Saturn on your planet. Aren't they still here?"

"No." Dr. Davinchy was subdued. He hated to think that the Moonsters knew more about the history of the Earth than he did. Kalmuck made scoffing noises, but Dr. Davinchy silenced him, and continued. "Be that as it may, Matt, the population of our planet is yelling their heads off at the scientists, politicians, and journalists, wanting to know just what this is all about. And now, to make things worse, the SPUFOS have arrived."

"The SPUFOS?"

"They belong to the Society for the Protection of Unidentified Flying Objects. This is the chance they've been waiting for, to catch a UFO on the ground."

Matt waved his hand at the *Feebey*'s interior. "You mean this is an unidentified flying object?"

Dr. Davinchy smiled. "That's what it is called, until it's identified. Now, all we'd like to have you do is hold a press conference, where we can get everything out in the open, and then you folks can get on your way again."

"A press conference?"

"It's simple. You don't have to say anything, except answer a few questions."

And that is how Commander Matthew Looney and Vice-Chairman Heckity got introduced to that fine old earthly custom. The press conference wasn't as simple as Dr. Davinchy had promised. It was a noisy and crowded affair. The two Moonsters sat at a table in the main cabin of the *Feebey,* and the Earthlings faced them. Before it started Matt was pestered by those who wanted him to write about his experiences for magazines, newspapers, and book publishers. He took note of their offers and promised to let them know. Other commercial opportunities came his way, and he had to turn them down because of Space Navy regulations. The press conference finally began, and through questions and answers the story unfolded which is well known to those who have studied Cosmic History in school: about Matt's earlier visits to Earth, about the unauthorized landings and approaches by earthships in Moon territory, about the hijacking of the space trekkers by Dr. Davinchy and Kalmuck, and then, finally, the cat was out of the bag.

Ratchet A. Keyhole, a founder of SPUFO, had the floor. The record shows that the testimony went like this:

KEYHOLE: Commander Looney, suh, we at the Society fo' the protection o' unahdentifahd flyin' objecks, is etuhnally grateful to you-all fo' makin' this heah trip to ouah li'l ol' planet. Fo' yeahs we-uns been made fun of by th' rest o' th' world fo' insistin' they's flyin' sauces out in space. Naow the folks around heah is eatin' crow lak it ain't nevah bin et befo' an' as the leadin' SPUFO, Ah wants to say: Welcome, and y'all come back soon, heah?

MATT: As I explained, Mr. Keyhole, our ships have explored many corners of the Universe,

"Fo' yeahs we-uns been made fun of."

and we've probably come close enough to Earth so you've seen us go by once in a while. Congratulations to your club for being so alert.

KEYHOLE: Well, naow, that's matty nass o' yew. They's sumpin' we's wondrin' about. Seems they's still one o' yo' ships circlin' ouah globe. Kin yew explain whuffo it's doin' that?

MATT: (*Uneasy. He glances at Heckity. They whisper. Matt nods and then speaks.*) Oh, that's nothing. It's just a kind of—well, I guess you'd call it a protective satellite. It's our—our Lava-Four, and it's hardly worth paying any attention to.

VOICE: May I? (*Matt gives the floor to a gentleman in the rear.*) I am A. A. Onestone, astronomer, and I was going to ask about that, too. How come all your Moonsters were screaming and yelling so, when the thing went over yesterday?

MATT: Heh, heh. They're happy, that's why.

KALMUCK (*leaping to his feet*): Why don't you admit it, Looney? That's the phony rocket that fizzled off from Crater Tycho, when you were trying to bulldoze me and Davinchy into thinking it was some secret weapon. Ho, ho!

MATT (*angered by Kalmuck's laughter, he blurts out the truth*): As usual, you're wrong, Kalmuck! The one we fired from Tycho went straight to its target, Eta Ursae Majoris. The Lava-Four that's circling your planet now is, I'm afraid, just as potent as that first one. I was hoping to keep this news from you Earthlings as long as possible.

KALMUCK: Aw, Looney, you give me a pain, with your silly—(*The rest of his words are drowned out by a piercing cry from the rear. It's the astronomer.*)

ONESTONE: Eta Ursae Majoris! (*Everyone turns to stare.*)

Tell me, sir, what happens when your Lava-Four reaches a target?

MATT: It vaporizes it.

ONESTONE: Then, perhaps that solves a stellar mystery.

DAVINCHY: What mystery?

ONESTONE: Not long ago, while you were away, half the handle of the Big Dipper just—it's hard to believe, and that's why we didn't make an official announcement—it just plain disappeared.

DAVINCHY: Half the handle?

ONESTONE: Of Ursa Major, The Great Bear, The Big Dipper. The star Benetnasch, or Eta of Ursa Major, as all astronomers know it. Eta Ursae Majoris, in Latin. The tail of the Great Bear, or the tip of the handle of the Dipper. Gone. Kaput.

KALMUCK: You sure, mister? I didn't see nothing of the sort.

ONESTONE: You can't observe the constellation from this part of the globe. But I assure you, my friend, the Big Dipper has been missing a piece of its handle for about a week.

KALMUCK (*clenching his fists, and growling at Matt*): Why you punks! Ruining our favorite, the Big Dipper. I oughta— (*He is so worked up he just chokes and his face gets redder than ever. He can't go on. Yet no one else speaks, either. The things they have learned at the press conference have been almost too much for the minds of the Earthlings. After all, they have learned in their schools that there is no life in the Universe except on Earth. Moonships, flying saucers—these are stories that are hard to prove. Now, here are intelligent visitors from another cosmic body. Finally a journalist is heard.*)

JOURNALIST: Commander Looney, if my notes are correct, you're telling us that a Lava-Four weapon of yours was sent on a mission to destroy that star.

MATT: It was a harmless way of showing you our strength.

JOURNALIST: And now there is a Lava-Four in orbit around Earth?

MATT: Yes, but that was a mistake. We didn't—

JOURNALIST: It could vaporize Earth, as it did the star?

MATT: Yes.

JOURNALIST: What's holding it back?

MATT: Well, nothing right now. It is supposed to drop its deadly cargo tomorrow some time. (*The Earthers are alarmed.*) But, wait, our finest scientists are working on the matter, so there's nothing to worry about. Let's see, it's time for them to send in their report right now. I'll break a regulation and let you folks listen in on the message. (*Matt goes to the Spectrophone and starts it up. The audience becomes restless. Dr. Davinchy tries to calm them.*)

DAVINCHY: Now, please quiet down, everyone. These Moon scientists are very competent.

I know that from experience. Quiet, here it comes! (*Everyone concentrates on the Spectrophone screen. Admiral Looney comes on.*)

ADMIRAL: Matt, here is the report I promised you on how to prevent the Lava-Four from making its deadly plunge downward, thus exploding its helio-activated lava all over the globe.

MATT (*impatiently*): Yes, yes, what do we do?

ADMIRAL: There is no way to stop the bomb.

MATT: But—but—

ADMIRAL: I suggest you get your travelers back into their spaceships as quickly as possible and resume your voyage to Hercules. You see, Matt, the Earth and all its inhabitants are doomed.

13. Matt Is Put On the Spot

Word that your planet is about to be turned into gas, and you along with it, is pretty hard to swallow. The press conference had come to a close, and everyone was standing there talking, asking questions, or scratching their heads. A group had surrounded Matt, with Dr. Davinchy among them. He was probably the man who understood better than any how serious the situation was.

"Tell me, Matt, is this Lava-Four the same as the one you shot off at that star?" When Matt nodded, the Earth scientist asked, "What is the length of time it takes to work?"

"Well, from the way the Lava-Three used to

operate on asteroids and other little targets like that, I'd guess that after the Four hits the Earth, it will be a long time before the compressed lava spreads completely around the globe and suffocates it. You see, this lava picks up energy from native rocks as it goes along. It will be a slow process, but a sure one. There will be no way to halt it."

There was a chuckle from Ratchet A. Keyhole. "Yo-all is pullin' mah laig."

Before Matt could say more, Wiley Kalmuck pushed his way into the forefront. The others had fallen silent, and the skinny Earthman's warning rang through the spaceship. "If this is the truth, Buster, you got a peck of trouble comin' your way! Just tell me, what do you propose to do about the mess you got us into?"

"Mr. Kalmuck, I am as upset by this turn of events as you are. But my first duty is to the members of my party, and my orders are to abandon this ugly planet to its fate, as much as it saddens me."

Kalmuck backed up, spread his arms out wide and pushed his fellow Earthers away. He spread his legs and dropped his big hands to his hips. It was then that Matt saw that he was wearing a sidearm. Kalmuck's fingers twitched as his right hand inched toward the holster. "Them's fightin' words, pardner!" he snarled. "Make your move."

Matt froze. He knew that if he made the move, toward the solar gun he was wearing, that Kalmuck would draw. He also knew that the Code of the Cosmos ruled that neither could draw till the other had. The crowd had flattened themselves against the bulkheads of the cabin, or dropped to the deck to avoid the flying bullets that they expected. Time stood still as the two faced each other. Matt was not afraid for his own safety, because he was a crack shot, but he feared that someone else might suffer. Besides, he had no wish to hurt Kalmuck, despite his miserable behavior.

"Whassa matter?" Kalmuck taunted Matt. "Yella?"

That made Matt angry, just as Kalmuck hoped it would, and he was close to the point of accepting the challenge, even though he knew it would be a mistake, when there was a shout from outside the cabin door. "Here she comes!" came a yell in the language of the Moon. It was followed by cries of terror. For a fraction of a second Kalmuck's eyes flickered at the unexpected noise. That was all Matt needed. Almost as fast as the speed of light his hand whipped the gun from his side and pressed its trigger. Aiming instinctively, Matt sent a solar pellet straight to the butt of his antagonist's gun. At the same moment Kalmuck slapped leather, but the superheated hydrogen pellet had melted the gun to the holster, and the weapon was stuck. Belt, holster, and all became tangled around his waist as he grappled with them.

All this had taken place in an instant. With Matt's superb marksmanship, the spell was broken, and the mob surged outside and down the ladder to find out what the Moonster's cries meant. They shoved Kalmuck along with them. As they reached the ground, they were just in time to see an awful sight overhead: the great thundering Lava-Four bomb was passing by. Smoke and flames poured from its engines, which rumbled as it progressed slowly through the heavens. Moonsters and Earthlings alike were afraid now, as all were aware of the missile's deadly cargo. The screams and cries were worse than ever. Moonsters ran for their spaceships. Earthlings scattered across the plain, headed for their airplanes. Matt and Vice-Chairman Heckity watched the scene from the *Feebey*'s spaceshield.

"Whew!" Heckity wiped his brow. "I can see what you mean about these people. They are crazy! Tell me, Commander, how were you going to get out of that showdown with the Earthman?"

Matt scratched his chin. "I haven't the least idea, but I am sure glad that Lava bomb came along."

Heckity grabbed Matt's arm in a tight grip. "Commander! That's the last pass before the bomb falls! We've got to get going, and fast!"

"Easy does it, Heckity. We've been on the alert for two days. As soon as I give the word, we'll blast right off. First, though, I have a little something to attend to."

"What's that?"

"I want to say farewell to one of my Earthling friends."

"Well, make it snappy, Commander, and in the meantime, we shall batten down the hatches and prepare to take off."

"Right you are. Have the roll taken and make sure everyone is accounted for. Don't forget that the Flight Librarian is in the Outback on a field trip with her pupils, trying to keep them from getting the jitters."

Vice-Chairman Heckity hurried away to perform his errands. Matt called Mr. Bones to make ready for blast-off, then checked his solar gun, climbed down the ladder to the ground and started across the desert toward the Earthmen's encampment. He had taken only a few steps when he stopped: the airplanes were flying away, one after the other. The Earthlings were deserting the Outback. But then Matt spied a lone figure kicking up dust as it came his way. *I hope it isn't Kalmuck,* he thought, and he loosened his gun. It wasn't. It turned out to be Leonard O. Davinchy, the very man Matt was looking for. The good doctor held out his hand. The Moonster grasped it.

"I came to say good-bye, my boy," the scientist said with a grim smile. "I don't like to think this is the end, but if it is, so be it. It's been nice knowing you, through this adventure and the others we've had together."

"No hard feelings, I hope, Doctor. I wish it could have been different." Suddenly Matt pulled his friend closer and whispered. "Listen,

I've got an idea. I'll look the other way while you stow away for Hercules. How about it? We could use a good Earth scientist like yourself. Come on, what do you say?"

"Tush, tush, Matt, forget it. I couldn't save my own skin and leave my fellow Earthers in the lurch. I am grateful for your concern, though."

"You're very brave."

"Not at all. I'm simply facing the facts, which is more than I can say for the rest of the world, from what I hear on the radio. People are locking themselves in bomb shelters. Some are in panic, rushing to banks and taking out all their money. Some of the prisons have been thrown open. Other Earthers are just going about their business as usual, and I can't blame them. After all, the end of the world has been predicted so many times through our history—wrongly—that they think it's a joke."

"What are your plans?" Matt asked.

"My orders are to remain here, with Wiley Kalmuck and a small staff. We have to make reports back to headquarters about your activities. You see, when the end comes, we want to have it all on file."

"Keep Kalmuck away from me, or there'll be trouble."

"He's scraping leather off his gun. I warn you, Matt, he's out for revenge, and I can't stop him."

"We'll be taking off shortly, and I doubt he can do much in the meantime."

Not far from where this conversation was going on, Flight Librarian Maria Looney was returning from the field trip. The Brainpusher had given her a quick course in Terrestrial Flora and Fauna, and she led her pupils across the sandy, dry soil and told them about the Earth.

"This is an interesting land, children, unlike any other on this planet. There are unusual beasts, such as the duckbill platypus and the teddy bear, and strange trees like the scribbly gum and the black wattle. One of the nice things about the Outback, where we are now, is that there is no water, except deep under the ground. And, also, there are no meteor showers to worry about. Although the air isn't as pleasant to breathe as that nice vacuum back home, it certainly isn't poisonous, as a lot of Moonsters still believe." Maria looked ahead of her and saw her brother and Dr. Davinchy. Behind them loomed the shape of the *Feebey*. As she approached, Matt spoke to her.

"Well, Sis, how did it go?"

"Oh, it was marvelous, Matthew. We've learned a lot, but there is much more to see on this planet. It would be nice if we could come back some day. I'd like to take a class to the ancient pyramids of Egypt and to modern cities like Peking and—"

Matt was surprised. "How do you know about all those subjects?"

Maria smiled happily. "From the Brainpusher. It's really the most wonderful invention. I've been cramming all sorts of knowledge into me. It's so exciting."

Turning to the little ones, Matt urged them toward the spaceships. "All right, children, get aboard the School Rocket now. We're going to take a nice, long voyage in a moonit." The kids wandered on, and Matt spoke to his sister. "You won't be making a return trip to see Peking, I'm afraid. Before long this planet will be no more."

"What? You mean—the Lava-Four can't be stopped, as you promised it would?" Matt nodded. Maria saw the look on Dr. Davinchy's face. A strange expression came into her eyes. She seemed suddenly frightened. "Wait a moonit. I'm thinking of something." She shivered.

"Are you all right?" her brother asked. "What's the matter?"

She closed her eyes, and the pretty pale face turned to green. She slumped to the ground and lay there in a heap. Matt knelt down and raised her by the shoulders. "Maria!" She didn't answer. He carried her to where the *Feebey* stood. Some of the children and grown-ups gathered in a little circle. "Quick, a cup of canal juice!" Matt ordered, and it was brought from the ship's galley. Maria sipped it, and her eyelids fluttered. She saw Matt and sat up, apparently quite alarmed.

"You mustn't leave! You must halt the Lava-Four! Their lives depend upon it!"

Matt tried to calm her. "We've been through this, Sis. There's no way to save the Earthers. They will have to rescue themselves. We shall have enough of a problem getting our own Moonsters away safely. Now, come on, pull yourself together and let us be on our way before the holocaust."

"Quick, a cup of canal juice!"

Maria took hold of Matt's arm. Her voice faltered. "I'm talking about our own kind, those on the Moon. Mother and Dad and the others. If the Lava-Four destroys the Earth, we shall never see them again."

Matt sighed. "Come on, stop the nonsense and let's get going. The Earth is doomed, and that's the whole unhappy story." He pulled the girl to her feet and tried to make her go to her spaceship. She held back.

"Listen, Matthew," she declared hoarsely, gripping his arm, "bodies attract each other—with a force—that varies directly—as the product of their masses—and inversely as the square of the distance between them."

"—and inversely as the square of the distance between them!" It was Dr. Leonard O. Davinchy, chiming in with the same mysterious words.

"So?" Matt said. "What in heck does that mean?"

"Holy jumping Jehoshaphat!" cried Dr. Davinchy, slapping his forehead. "I never thought of that. Oh, Matt, are you ever in a pickle now! Ho, ho, ho! I'm sorry, I can't help but laugh. It's so sad it's funny."

"What in heaven's name are you talking about?" the puzzled Moonster demanded.

"This." Maria picked up a stick and traced some figures in the sand:

$$F = G\ \frac{Mm}{r^2}$$

"*F* is the force of attraction between Earth and Moon, and large *M* is the mass of Earth and small *m* the mass of Moon. Do away with large *M*, and *F* is reduced accordingly. In this case, to practically nothing."

Vice-Chairman Heckity had been listening to the conversation. "Could you please put that in simple language for us, Miss Looney?"

"I think so, sir. Now, here on Earth there is a powerful force that makes it difficult for us to walk around." She pointed to the *F*.

"Yes."

"The same force is what keeps our Moon in its place in the Universe, in its orbit around the Earth, and the Earth around the Sun. If we destroy this ugly planet, that will let the Moon go flying off into the solar system and goodness knows what will become of it." With the stick she crossed out the *F*, and then kicked sand over the other figures. Heckity, Matt, and the others who had heard were stunned into silence. Then her brother asked, "How do you know all this?"

"It came to me, that's all. I worked it out myself sort of automatically, from what I know after falling asleep the other day with the Brainpusher on the red Science ball. My head has been really going full speed since then. I can tell you lots more, like light refractions are the product of—"

"You've told us enough, young lady," Heckity interrupted. "If you're right, we're in trouble."

"Do you think she's right?" Matt asked.

"The Brainpusher has never been wrong before," Heckity said.

"I don't know about your Brainpusher, but I do know that Isaac Newton was right," Dr. Davinchy remarked. "That's his Law of Gravitation."

"What will happen?" Matt asked the Earth scientist.

"Well, let's see. It's something we've never really studied." Dr. Davinchy thought a moment. "Newton's laws would apply, of course. The Moon's momentum would carry it along for a period of time. It would flop around erratically until, sooner or later, it was captured by another larger body."

"Which larger body?"

"Hmmm. It could be Venus or Mars, if either of them were in the vicinity at the right time. But most likely it would be the Sun."

"So our Moon would go into another orbit," Matt suggested.

"Maybe. And maybe not."

"What is that supposed to mean?" Matt demanded.

The Earthling hesitated, then replied with a sad shake of his head. "Well, the chances are that your tiny Moon, without the Earth's influence, would be drawn closer and closer to the huge star we call the Sun, finally crashing into it and, of course, being destroyed."

Matt's shoulders sagged. He closed his eyes as though to erase the nightmare from his mind. He looked at Heckity. "We have no choice. The Earth is finished, and so is our beloved Moon."

A few Moonsters who had heard the prediction set up a fearful wailing and moaning, and the horrible news spread throughout the area. Vice-Chairman Heckity turned to Matt, his expression grim. "Commander, we do have a choice. That is to prevent this Earth from being melted by red-hot lava."

"But Mr. Heckity, we tried, and we failed."

Heckity's voice was firm and loud. He stuck out his chin. "You're in charge here! Try again! And come up with something—fast!"

14. Maria Gets an Idea

Stranded on the ugliest planet in the Universe with a problem that seemed insoluble, Commander Matthew M. Looney sat in the pilot's seat of the *Feebey,* his head in his hands, thinking, *I sure wish I had a simple job in the powder factory right now. Poor Mom and Dad. And all my friends. Doomed.* Matt began to choke. Then he took a grip on himself. *What's this? I'm not going to cry, am I? Pull yourself together, Looney, and get on with it.* He stood up and started pacing the deck, his brain working at top speed.

The first order of business was to get a full description of Lava-Four. With that in mind, he ordered Mr. Bones to put in a call to the Moon. Vice-Chairman Heckity had gone to speak to the assembled Moonsters to explain this latest development. Maria was in her cabin resting, after her mental ordeal, and weeping softly to herself over the impending disaster. Dr. Davinchy had returned to the Earthmen's camp on the other side of the landing area, where he told his colleagues what was about to happen.

When Matt finally talked to Professor Ploozer, the scientist said, "My gegoodness! And we always thought it was the other way around."

"What do you mean?"

"That formula. We decided that it was the Moon that keeps the Earth in place."

"Well, you've been wrong. I talked to Dr. Davinchy and he proved it. Says a friend of his named Isaac Newton discovered it. No time to argue, anyway. I want you to send me a complete description of the Lava-Four."

"Why, Matthew, I've getold you there's no way to stop the bomb. Besides, it's getop secret. I'm not allowed to tell you how it works."

"Professor Ploozer!" Matt shouted. "We're all in this together, you and us. Give me the information or you'll end up burned to a crisp!"

Professor Ploozer frowned. "Well, I guess it's all right this one time." It wasn't long before the printing machine on the *Feebey* Spectrophone started clicking, and a detailed drawing of the Lava-Four appeared. Matt grabbed it and studied it. There wasn't much time. The bomb was in its fourth orbit.

"What's this guidance sensor?" he asked.

"That is what steers it. She gorbits the Earth four times while the guidance sensor warms up, and then it gradually turns down and aims the bomb toward the ground."

"Then what?" Matt asked.

"The flint is gesmashed back into the secret formula, and the red-hot lava goes geblooey—all over the place! Oh, it's really the most marvelous sight. I wish I could be there to see it."

Matt was disgusted. "You'll see it, all right, and it'll be the last thing you'll see if I don't figure out something, and fast."

"Why, Matthew, we geput our heads together and couldn't come up with anything. What makes you gethink you can?"

"Because I must, that's what. And when a Looney makes up his mind to do something, he usually does it. Besides, I don't think you tried very hard. Now that we know that our own Moon is threatened, it's more important."

"Well, good gluck."

After asking the Professor to stand by at all times in case he was needed, Matt turned off the Spectrophone. He immediately called together all Moonsters with any scientific training, and put them to work on the problem. He even sent a drawing of the bomb to Dr. Davinchy, begging him and his fellow Earthmen to help. As the day wore on, Moonsters argued and offered their ideas. Go on to Hercules now, some said. Return home, others said, so all Moonkind will face the future together—whatever it might be. The Earthmen could only think of shooting down the Lava-Four with another missile, but Matt explained that it would explode the bomb that much sooner.

Robinson K. Russo's feelings were made known as he paraded around with a sign on the end of a long stick:

LOWER THE BOOM.
THERE'S PLENTY OF ROOM.
IF THE MOON FLIES AWAY,
WE'LL FIND IT SOME DAY.

Although Moonsters are slow to anger, this was almost too much, from the fellow who had caused all the trouble in the first place. A gang of Moonsters chased Russo, shouting, "Hang him!" until he took refuge in his spaceship.

Matt's own ideas weren't any better than anyone else's. He stared at the drawing again and again, using the astroputer to make calculations, but no solution made sense. He got more and more pessimistic; in fact he was getting kind of frightened. He heard his name called. It was his sister, Maria. She climbed into the *Feebey*'s cabin. She looked tired.

"I've been trying to sleep," she said. "But I couldn't, thinking about those poor people back home. What have you decided to do?"

"Nothing," grumbled Matt. "Things look hopeless."

"What's that you're reading?" Matt handed her the sketch of the bomb. She pointed to the parts. "What's this? And what's that do?"

Matt described the bomb for her. "Too bad you can't put that Brainpusher to work figuring things out for us," he said.

"Hmmm. This gadget out front—"

"The guidance sensor?"

"Yes, Why don't you just push it so it points away from the Earth and then the Lava-Four will go in another direction?"

Matt sighed. "In the first place, the Earth's gravity slowly bends it down. We could push it up, but it would soon turn down again. In the second place, I'm standing here and the bomb is away up there."

"Can't you fly up there in the *Feebey* and go alongside if you wanted to?" Maria asked.

"I suppose so, but there wouldn't be enough fuel to come back here and then take off again for Hercules."

"Why come back?"

Matt looked puzzled.

"I mean," she explained, "you could go on to Hercules from there. You don't need much fuel once you get started. And we could follow."

Matt nodded his head slightly. "Yeah, I guess you're right. So what do I do when I catch her?"

Maria's eyes brightened as she told Matt her plan. "Can you get out of the *Feebey* while in flight? Can you go onto the Lava-Four and make adjustments and stuff like that?"

"Sure. I've got a vacuum suit and all the equipment."

"Well, you creep out onto the front of the bomb and you fix this guidance business so that it never aims at the planet."

"I've already told you—"

"Yes, yes," Maria went on excitedly. "But you attach a little anti-gravity machine to it, and then no matter what happens, it will never be attracted to the Earth. Now, what do you think of that?" She stood back and grinned at him.

Matt made a face. "It'll never work, that's what I think of it."

"Why not?"

"Because, the—um—well—I—it's—" Matt stuttered along like that and finally admitted, "Maybe it's worth a try."

Maria clapped her hands joyously.

"So where do we get the little AGM?" Matt asked.

"Everybody's got one. Just borrow it."

"Not so easy," he said. "Each person needs his, or he can't move. It won't be borrowing as much as taking it for good. I have to have mine or I'm no good to the expedition. You need yours. When—if—we get to Hercules, we may need them, too. So who is so unimportant that

Maria began to smile, too.

it doesn't matter if he can't walk around any more." Suddenly a smile appeared on his face.

Maria looked into his eyes and she began to smile, too. "If you're thinking what I'm thinking," Matt said, "come on, let's go."

He took Maria's arm and they hurried toward the spaceships. They spied the one that had HERCULES OR BUST! painted on the side. A gang of Anti-Earthers were lounging around at the foot of the gangway. As they approached, Matt whispered into his sister's ear, "Keep them busy." The Moonsters stood up as the Looneys came near. "Don't get up, men," Matt said. "I just want to confer with Mr. Russo about matters." He climbed up to the entrance.

As he went inside, he heard Maria say, "I had the most interesting experience with the Brainpusher yesterday . . ."

Opening the hatch, Matt stepped into the ship. It was dimly lit. *I've got to play this by by ear,* he thought. *If I ask Russo for his AGM, he is going to refuse. Where am I? Ah, the pilot house. Look at the empty cups. Been having another party. Nobody here. Go aft. Where's his cabin. Dark. Here's a door. What's it say? "Mr. Russo. Private."*

Matt knocked. He waited. There was no answer. He put his ear against the panel and heard a grinding noise. In and out, up and down. For an instant Matt wondered what it could be and then suddenly it dawned on him: snoring! Russo must be in there, sleeping off the effects of too much firmament. Matt carefully turned the handle and slowly pushed the door open. The hinges creaked, and the snoring stopped. Matt froze, half in the darkened cabin. There was some rustling and the snoring began again. Matt relaxed and approached the bunk. At one end he saw a large lumpy shape: Russo's head.

Now to find his anti-gravity machine. Most Moonsters had gotten in the habit of removing the AGM when they slept because it was uncomfortable. Matt felt around the bulkhead near the sleeper but couldn't find one. It couldn't be far away, because it would be difficult for him to get into his bunk without it. *He must be wearing it,* Matt guessed. His fingers went gently to the fellow's belt. There it was! He started loosening the four thumbscrews that held the device. He had three undone and was turning the last when the snoring stopped and Russo's voice muttered, "Who's there? Wha's happening?"

Matt's fingers worked furiously at the screw.

"Stop, thief!" yelled the leader of the Anti-Earth League. His hands reached out to grab Matt. But the AGM was loose, and Matt pulled it off Russo's belt and skedaddled out of the room. He tucked the little gadget into a pocket.

Russo's voice boomed after him as he hurried up the companionway toward the bridge.

"Hey, I can't lift my head. I'm stuck. My AGM! It's stolen! Help!"

Gravity held Russo down. Matt heard a thump. *Probably the poor guy falling to the deck,* Matt thought. *Too bad, but he got us into this mess in the first place.* Russo's cries faded away as Matt left the spaceship. He climbed down the ladder, where Maria was surrounded by some young fellows. One of them turned to Matt.

"Did I hear someone shouting in there?" he asked.

"Oh, yes," Matt smiled. "That was Mr. Russo, telling me how pleased he is with the way things are going. He wants you to get your engines warmed up; we're taking off for Hercules shortly."

The other fellow smiled and Matt called to

his sister. "Come on, Maria, we've got work to do." She excused herself and the two of them hurried away.

"Did you get it?" she asked him.

He patted his pocket. "Sure did. Now, on with the next phase of my plan."

She stopped in her tracks. "Whose plan?"

He grabbed her arm and pulled her along. "Okay, our plan—well, *your* plan."

15. Stopping the Mighty Lava Bomb

It was nighttime in the Outback. Some Moonsters were in their bunks. The youngsters slept, but those old enough to know were tossing and turning as they thought about Matt's mission. Some stood on the darkened plain and hopefully waited for the *Feebey* to take off. Lights burned brightly inside the great Moonship, where Matt and his staff rehearsed the scheme. Matt climbed into the vacuum suit, while mechanics tested all the working parts to see that they were in order. The special double hatch, which would let him out into space, was oiled and checked carefully.

The key to the plan was not only Russo's AGM, but an ingenious clamp which Mr. Bones had constructed. It was a simple device, operated with one hand, which would make it possible for Matt to attach the anti-gravity gadget to the guidance sensor. Matt practiced the move again and again until he guessed he could manage it with his eyes closed, if he had to.

Finally, the young Commander spoke to the others. "Well, ready to go?"

"Ready if you are," Mr. Bones replied.

"Then sound general quarters, and prepare to get under way."

"Aye, aye, sir." The mate relayed the orders to the rest of the ship and there was a hustle and bustle as the crew went to stations for the fateful flight. Matt turned to Vice-Chairman Heckity.

"Let's go over the plan once more," he told the official. "I'll have completed the job before sunrise. The *Feebey* will not have enough fuel to return to Earth and make another takeoff. You will wait here with the other Moonships until you hear from me. When you get my signal, blast off and join me at the rendezvous point near the asteroid Geographos. Then, on to Hercules!"

"You can count on me, Commander. Good luck." The Vice-Chairman gripped Matt's hand

and then departed down the gangway. The *Feebey* was buttoned up; her engines roared, and the spacecraft lifted off the ground and moved in the direction of the Milky Way. Matt was at the wheel, while Mr. Bones sat at the console of the mighty astroputer, gathering information about the path of the Lava-Four in its orbit around Earth. It would be necessary to locate the bomb and steer the *Feebey* quickly to intercept it. The deadly weapon was already in its fourth orbit; every moment counted. This was so complicated that, without the astroputer, it would take days for a navigator to plot a course. Right now the marvelous machine was purring and her lights twinkled. Mr. Bones knew that all he had to do was to feed into it some facts about the time of takeoff of the *Feebey,* her speed, and her weight, plus similar facts about the Lava-Four, and the astroputer would tell all. He did that, and as the tape clicked out the figures, Mr. Bones typed them onto the blank card of the automatic pilot, and slipped the card into its slot. Matt took his hands off the wheel. A very slight movement of the nose of the ship and a change in the sound of the motors told him that automation had taken over. *If all goes well,* he thought, *we shall meet the Lava-Four before she starts her deadly plunge to the Earth.* He looked through the spaceshield and saw the distant shapes of the other Moonships, waiting on the Outback flatland.

"Let's go," he said to his mate. Mr. Bones got the vacuum suit for Matt and held it while he put it on, except for the helmet, which he would don at the last moment. The gloves fitted Matt's fingers very tightly, so that he would have no trouble using them. He held the clamp, one end of which was attached to Russo's AGM, and the other end of which would fit the guidance sensor of the Lava-Four. He practiced squeezing the levers which would cause the clamp to grip the sensor.

"Remember Professor Ploozer's warning," Mr. Bones reminded him. "Don't touch the sensor and the flint detonator at the same time or else—"

"Don't worry. What's our position now?" Matt licked his lips. He was getting slightly nervous.

"Better get set, Commander."

Mr. Bones then put the helmet on Matt's head and locked it there. Through the spaceshield their eyes searched the dark sky. An object approached. It was the Lava-Four.

"Take her off automatic," Matt said through his speaker. "Go alongside, but not too close."

Mr. Bones nodded and did as he was ordered. He steered the *Feebey* by hand, and instructed the engine room to slow engines, for the bomb traveled at a reduced rate of speed. While he held her on course, Matt went to the exit chamber. He turned and waved good-bye to Mr. Bones, who gave him the thumbs-up sign and smiled. Matt felt for the clamp and AGM at his belt, turned and entered the chamber, locking himself in. Then he opened the hatch that let him out into space. He pressed the GO button on his little rocket, and shot out into the black, chilly void. He quickly adjusted his speed with the throttle, guiding himself in the direction of the giant bomb that floated along in front of him. He looked back and saw Mr. Bones's anxious face lit up in the cockpit of the *Feebey*. The Earth was half dark and half light. Somewhere down there the Moonships were warming up. Cosmic rays tapped his suit—pockety-pock.

Better get to work. Look at that thing. Full of compressed lava. Hot. No, it's cold. Hot when it ignites. Wonder how it works. Oh, well, who cares? Closer. Watch out! Flint. Hey, what's happening? The sensor has bent! Maybe it's beginning its dive. Quick. Take hold gently. Turn it up. It bends easily. Oops, not too far. Gee, I can steer the bomb. Hmmm. Here, now for the AGM. Let's see, clamp it on the nose. Squeeze this. Let go. There.

Matt backed off to watch the behavior of the deadly weapon now that he had attached the AGM to its guidance sensor. He floated along at the same speed as the Lava-Four, noting that the sensor stuck out in front as straight as could be. After a few moments Matt observed there was no change in direction of the bomb, and he realized he had done all he could. He had a confident feeling deep inside that he had been successful. He twisted the throttle of his rocket motor and flew back toward the *Feebey*. He made his way into the compression chamber, locked the hatch behind him and let himself into the ship through the door.

Mr. Bones and other members of the crew were there to greet him. They quickly removed the helmet from his head and cried out their congratulations to him.

"Good work, Commander!" exulted the mate. The others echoed his sentiments and shook Matt's hand or patted him on the back as they helped him out of the vacuum suit. Matt couldn't help grinning, for he was indeed pleased, too, at the way things were turning out.

"Thank you, men," he said. "But we've got a long road ahead of us. On to Hercules."

"On to Hercules," were the happy shouts, as the crew went back to their posts.

"Mr. Bones," Matt said, "steer a course for the asteroid Geographos, while I report the happy tidings to Space Control at home and to Vice-Chairman Heckity and our loyal and patient followers in the Outback."

Dawn was breaking when the Moonsters on Earth heard the joyful news. Vice-Chairman Heckity, after receiving it from Matt over the Spectrophone, made the announcement over the loudspeakers. Everyone rushed out of the ships and onto the desert, embracing each other and shouting and crying in happiness. When we say everyone, we mean almost everyone. A strange sight appeared in the midst of the celebration: it was the big cranium of Robinson K. Russo, tipped to one side, as he rode piggyback on his young, strong son, Enrico K. Russo. The boy pushed his way to the forefront of the gathering, where his father shouted at Vice-Chairman Heckity:

"Oh, it's fine for you to cheer and be pleased! But what about me, without my anti-gravity machine? How am I supposed to get along? Look, I can't walk, or even hold my head up. I want my AGM back, or one just like it, or else—"

"Or else what?" Heckity asked.

"Or else you'll find out," Russo said mysteriously.

"Well," Heckity said. "There are no more AGM's, and so we can't help you."

"Oh!" Russo cried loudly in rage. "That does it! Enrico, take me away from here. Remember, Heckity, I warned you!"

As the angry fellow was carried out of sight, the Moonsters went on with their celebration. Little did they dream of the diabolical revenge that Russo had in mind. He, the dyed-in-the-wool Anti-Earther, had decided to join the other side.

16. Farewell to Earth

A campfire burned itself down to embers in the Outback. Around it the Earthmen slept, rolled up in blankets or sleeping bags. From where the many Moonships rested, the red glow could be seen faintly in the darkness. Enrico K. Russo staggered through the soft sand, as his father urged him on. The young fellow had turned his own AGM up to D, the strongest setting, but still he had trouble toting the load. Moonsters' muscles were just not powerful enough to put them on equal terms with the Earth's gravity.

"Faster, faster!" Russo said from his son's back.

"Have mercy, Pop, I'm going as fast as I can."

The noise they made was enough to awaken one of the sleepers, Wiley Kalmuck, who got to his feet and drew a gun. Then the others got up, too.

"All right, hold it right there," he ordered.

But Enrico couldn't have moved another step, anyway. He fell to his knees while Robinson K. Russo rolled off and flopped down on his back. He immediately started shouting, his face aimed at the heavens.

"Who's in charge around here?"

"Well, now, little feller," Kalmuck said, "I reckon you could say that was me. Now just get up on your feet and tell old Wiley what this is all about." He lifted the limp figure up easily, but when he let go, Russo slumped to the ground again.

"His AGM's been stolen," Enrico explained. "He can't stand."

"Matt Looney took it," Russo said bitterly, "and that's what I wanted to tell you. He's fixed the Lava-Four so it won't drop on the Earth." He described how Matt had done it.

Kalmuck showed surprise. The other Earthmen perked up their ears. Dr. Davinchy climbed out of his sleeping bag. "Is that true?" he asked. "Is that why the Moonship took off last night?" Both the Russos nodded. "Boy, that's a relief," the Earthman sighed.

The elder Russo spoke again.

"Listen, I'll make a deal with you. You get me an AGM and I'll let you in on all sorts of secrets, like how the engines of our spaceships work—remember, you were interested in that? —and where's the best place to land on the Moon, and how many Lava-Three's we have, and—"

"Whoa, there, feller," Kalmuck interrupted. "You mean, you're gonna do a little spying for us? And all I have to do is swipe one of them AGM's for you?"

Dr. Davinchy broke in, "Wiley, I don't think that's such a good idea. It's certainly not the best way to start off diplomatic relations with a foreign body. Besides, we got a look at the device on Matt's previous trip to Earth."

"That's right, but this is the new, improved AGM, I hear, and for scientific purposes, maybe we ought to get hold of one of these here gadgets. We could really go places if we knew what makes it tick. What d'ya say, Doc?"

"Oh, I think that would be rather difficult," the scientist replied.

"What d'ya mean? The kid, here, has one." Kalmuck took a step toward Enrico, who immediately started running.

"Oh, no, you don't!" he shouted as he disappeared from the scene.

"My goodness," Kalmuck snickered, "jittery rascal, ain't he? We'll soon see about this." He took out his gun, twirled the cylinder to check its ammunition, and started after Enrico. Daylight was gathering, and the shapes of the Moon vessels were visible in the distance. But before Wiley Kalmuck had gone very far he was halted by a cry from the Russo who had not fled.

"Stop! Don't leave me here. Take me with you. I must be returned to my spaceship. And don't take Enrico's AGM. Get someone else's. He's my son."

Kalmuck looked down at the supine figure. "Who d'ya think you are, Buster, givin' orders to Wiley Kalmuck, Secret Agent?"

"Who am I? My good man, just because I happen to be flat on my back doesn't mean I am not a personage of some importance. I am Robinson K. Russo, former Member of Mongress, and ex-Mayor of Crater Arzachel. I am Chairman of the Sea of Clouds Evaporation Committee and I also happen to be President of the League of Anti-Ear—um, skip that—and I am Founder of the Solar Scouts of the Sky, and I hold the Order of the Green Gorgonzola as well as the Degree of Doctor of Lunacy, which I obtained when I was graduated from the Mooniversity with highest honors, and—"

"Enough!" cried Wiley Kalmuck. But Russo made the mistake of continuing.

"—and I daresay, sir, that my fellow traveling companions from the Moon will not leave here without me."

Kalmuck's eyes widened. "So they won't go without you, eh?" he smiled. A fiendish plot had formed within his crafty brain. "Then we'll keep you here as hostage. That will give us some bargaining power when we start making plans for more landings on the Moon. It will also give us the chance to get our mitts on one of those AGM's, and maybe some other fancy inventions that you Moon characters seem to be able to come up with so easily." He motioned to the Earthmen. "Keep an eye on him, you guys, while I do a little highfalutin negotiation. Heh,

heh, heh!" Kalmuck trotted toward the Moonships, his sly laughter ringing out in the crisp dawn.

He hadn't covered much ground before he saw the flames and heard the roar that meant a spaceship was taking off. One of them went into the sky, gathering speed. Then another followed, and another. Kalmuck ran faster, but he wasn't fast enough to get there before all the Moon vehicles except one had flown away. The one that remained had a small knot of Moonsters standing at the gangway. Enrico was one of them because, sure enough, it was the Russo space yacht that was still grounded.

"Someone's coming," Enrico said to his fellow Moonsters. "Maybe they're bringing Pop. No, it's an Earthman, alone. Hey, it's that bad guy! He's armed, and he wants our AGM's! Quick, inside!" They all scrambled up the ladder and into the ship, slamming the hatch and locking it. Wiley Kalmuck sized up the picture at once, and started shooting at Enrico and his crew as they disappeared inside. The bullets missed and made ping-ping noises on the metal hull.

The Earthman stood at the foot of the ladder

and called out, "It's no use hiding, because you're all going to have to come out sooner or later. Can you hear me up there?"

Inside, Enrico K. Russo, who had taken command in his father's absence, answered through the loudspeaker, "Yes, we hear you. We're not giving up our AGM's."

Kalmuck called back. "Here's the deal, Buster. Deliver me one of them little gadgets if you want your famous Robinson K. Russo back, ex-member of Mongress, ex-Mayor of something-or-other and holder of the Green Watchamacallit, and so on and so forth *ad nauseam*. No AGM, no Russo. Take it or leave it. Also, you can get in touch with Looney and tell him to get his caravan back here lickety-split or else Russo will spend the rest of his days on Earth lying on his back. I'll give you time to think it over." With that Kalmuck leaned against the spaceship's engine pod and stuffed some chewing tobacco into his big mouth.

Shortly afterwards, Dr. Leonard O. Davinchy came along. After Wiley Kalmuck had told him about the ultimatum, Dr. Davinchy said, hesitantly, "Do you really think this is the wise thing to do?"

"Sure, sure. I know how sentimental these birds are about their fellow Moonsters. They'll do anything to get back this famous citizen Russo. He's still there, isn't he?"

"Sure, the fellows are watching him. He couldn't move if he wanted to."

Kalmuck spat on the ground. "Ah, revenge is sweet."

While the two Earthmen waited, the Interspatial Spectrophones were crackling back and forth. Enrico told Heckity what had happened, and then Matt found out about it. All the Moonships floated aimlessly in space while their leaders decided what to do. Enrico and his crew stayed shut up in their spaceship in the Outback, awaiting orders from above. Finally they came. The decision had been made. Wiley Kalmuck and Dr. Davinchy found out what it was when they heard a low grinding sound inside the Russo spaceship. It grew louder, and smoke began to spurt out of the exhaust right next to them. With a shriek Kalmuck jumped and started running.

"Get out of here! They're blasting off!"

Dr. Davinchy didn't have to be told. He raced out of the way of the flames. He and his partner

"They're blasting off!"

ran until they came to their campsite, where the other Earthmen stared up in the air at the last Moon craft to depart the Outback. Their reaction was mild compared to that of Robinson K. Russo. He lay on his back and watched his only chance of getting away disappear into the blue. He couldn't speak.

Dr. Davinchy shook his head. "I didn't think they'd do it. Abandon one of their own. But they must have had a good reason."

Wiley Kalmuck made a face. He threw his gun onto the dusty ground. "Well, you can't win 'em all. The lousy so-and-so's."

Finally Robinson K. Russo found his voice. "Oh, oh, oh, it's awful, awful. The terrible thing that has been done. We're sunk. It's the end."

Dr. Davinchy felt sorry for the stranded Moonster. He knelt down beside him and lifted his head. "Don't take on so, Mr. Russo. The Earth is a nice place, after you get used to it. Your leg muscles will strengthen, as time goes on, and you'll be walking and enjoying life just as much as the rest of us. I'm sure you'll be able to sell your story to the magazines—maybe even write a book—why, you'll be famous." He beamed at the unhappy chap.

But Russo wailed even more. "It isn't what you think. I don't want to stay here, for one very, very good reason. Oh, if I'd only told Matt Looney. I was so stubborn."

"Told him what?" asked the Earth scientist.

"About my anti-gravity machine, the one he attached to the bomb to keep it in orbit around the Earth."

"What about it?" Wiley Kalmuck said.

"I didn't take very good care of it," Russo moaned. "I dropped it and there's a crack in the inner chamber, the one that scrambles the ultra-mundane corpuscles and defies gravity. I never told anyone. But the thing sort of hiccups."

"Hiccups?" That was Dr. Davinchy.

"Yes. Every once in a while it stops working for a moonit or two."

"What does that mean, Doc?" Kalmuck demanded.

"If I understand correctly what Matt was up to, it means that every time the AGM hiccups, the Lava-Four will sneak a little bit closer to us."

"And some day," blubbered Russo, "there will be that last hiccup, and down she comes and—oh, oh, oh!"

"Hot lava?" Kalmuck asked.

"Hot, hot lava," Russo whispered hoarsely. "Earth is doomed."

Dr. Davinchy smiled. "Why, I thought that was the goal of your organization. You should be pleased."

Russo groaned from his position on the ground. "Not any more, sir, not any more. I have just formed a new organization. It's called the Save-the-Earth League."

The scientist chuckled. "Well, I'll tell you, Mr. Russo. I know a little something about ultra-mundane corpuscles, too, and with a powerful group like the Save-the-Earth League helping, I daresay we can cure a matter of a hiccup sooner or later."

"You better make it sooner, Doc," Kalmuck growled.

Dr. Davinchy didn't reply. He looked upward to the rocket trails of the space caravan that wound its way into the celestial void, bound toward the Hercules Globular Cluster. He raised a hand in farewell.